VAIN
EMPIRES

BRANDILYN COLLINS

VAIN EMPIRES

Cover photo by Brandilyn Collins
Author name logo by DogEared Design

ISBN-10: 0692723110
ISBN-13: 978-0692723111

Challow Press
212 W. Ironwood Dr., Suite D
#316
Coeur d'Alene, ID 83814

Beelzebub, plotting the temptation of Man:

"There is a place ... of some new race, called Man ...
Thither let us bend all our thoughts, to learn ... where
their weakness ...
Seduce them to our party,
that their God may prove their foe ...
Advise if this be worth attempting, or to sit in darkness
here, hatching vain empires."

--Paradise Lost, John Milton

Whoever conceals their sins does not prosper, but the one
who confesses and renounces them finds mercy.

--Proverbs 28:13

Let the wicked forsake their ways and the unrighteous
their thoughts. Let them turn to the Lord, and he will
have mercy on them, and to our God, for he will freely
pardon.

Isaiah 55:7

Prologue

The stage stood ready. Waiting for victims.

Sickly light from a bare overhead bulb filtered through the underground room, revealing floor and walls of concrete blocks. Four gray metal folding chairs. A square table in the center, supporting a small computer screen. In one corner of the room sat a half-sized refrigerator, holding bottled water and food. It emitted a low hum. In the opposite corner was a narrow door leading to a tiny bathroom. The toilet flushed. The sink had running water.

A nice touch. The *Dream Prize* producer smiled.

Fresh air pumped into the room through a vent in the ceiling.

On the front wall was a thick wooden door. A certain button pushed would open and close its digital lock. Beyond the door rose eighteen stairs, also dimly lit. They led to a second heavy door, this at ground level. Its lock — controlled by a similar button.

In time, as one grew accustomed to the bunker's low light, the round outline of an area cut high in the back wall would become visible. The hole was about three inches in diameter. What lay behind it was almost invisible yet deadly to the dreams of those trapped inside.

Sinners, they were, intent on hatching their vain empires. Sinners, all.

DREAM PRIZE

Day One

Sunday, March 6

Chapter 1

None of this mattered if she didn't win.

Not the transparent azure water, the alluring remote island with a large white wood house now in view, the warm ocean breeze under sunny skies. Not the five other mysterious contestants on the boat. Not the hard-faced captain who'd refused to talk, motioning them on board with a jut of his chin. Or the months Gina had hoped and prayed she would be chosen for the reality show. The exhilaration of learning she had. The long flight to Australia, leaving her husband, Ben, behind. The jet lag and sleepless previous night. The anticipation and dread now churning within her.

This lush beauty, the tears, the good and the bad—all of it was for one thing only. Ben's dream and hers.

Gina slid a hand across her lower belly.

Dream Prize. A fitting name for the reality show. Each contestant had been able to choose the prize he or she wanted. It could be money and/or gifts equaling up to ten million dollars. Or it could be something that money alone couldn't buy.

Gina would *win*.

The boat swayed, and warm spray misted on her sunglasses. She grabbed the railing.

They'd approached the small island by rounding its south side onto its western shore. Gina studied the house as it grew closer. Two storied and long, with a porch and upper deck, both running the entire length. White railing on the deck. White pillars on both levels. Much of the house was glass, upstairs and down. She couldn't wait to see the interior.

"That's one gussied-up house." Tori Hattinger, the attractive woman standing next to Gina at the boat railing, spoke the words almost to herself.

"Gussied up?"

Tori glanced at Gina, as if caught at something. "It's a Southern saying for being all dressed up."

"Oh." Gina couldn't detect an accent. "You from the South?"

"Maybe. Maybe not."

All right, be coy.

They'd been told little information about the challenges in *Dream Prize*. Gina did know the show had nothing to do with surviving the wild or eating worms or crazy physical tasks, which she never could have done. In fact they would live in luxury. Now that was more her style. Further, this game was a contest not of the body, but the mind. It focused in some way on finding out things about each other. The six contestants would earn points through their own deductions and from a voting TV audience. *"When you meet, tell each other nothing about yourself but your first and last names,"* read the terse welcome note in Gina's hotel room.

She had no problem with any of this. One thing Gina Corrales knew was how to read people. As a realtor, she had to. One look at a female client often told Gina how much the woman could afford to spend for a house. This one next to her — Tori — was probably mid-forties, five to six years older than she. Short, with chin-length bleached blonde hair and — were those brown eyes behind the sunglasses? She had a rich alto voice and looked fairly wealthy, given her blue designer shorts and silk top. Jimmy Choo sandals. No wedding ring, but a large blue sapphire on her right hand. Larger than usual diamond stud earrings. Her haircut and highlighting color job were well done. Nice skin and make-up and figure. Probably a size six — which made Gina's size eighteen feel all the larger. All those fine things cost money. Plus the woman oozed poise and confidence. Was she a doctor? Attorney? Businesswoman?

Gina glanced over her shoulder at the other female in their group — Shari Steele. Younger — maybe early twenties. Strikingly pretty, with dark brown hair to her shoulders. An oval face and great body. She wore red shorts and a clingy white shirt, which looked great against her tan. Had to be a size two, maybe even zero. Could be a model but not tall enough. She'd had her nails done recently in a black gel. A competitive air hung about her — something narrow-focused that seemed to go beyond merely winning this competition. And a touch of hardness, although underneath it Gina sensed a far less assured person than she wanted to appear. Shari stood steady-legged on the boat without holding on to anything, hands on her hips. Trying to look sure of herself.

Of the three male contestants, two of them were also young, maybe late twenties. Craig Emberly was average height, with a buzzed haircut and a long face. Not handsome but friendly-looking. He seemed to be enjoying every moment of their boat ride, as if he'd set off on a great adventure. He wore colorful board shorts, sandals, and a yellow T-shirt from Maui.

The second young man, Aaron Wang, was a tall, lean Chinese who spoke with no accent at all. Second generation, maybe? He was polite but ... removed. As if he held his emotions close to his chest. He spoke in terse sentences. Aaron wore blue shorts and a white knit shirt.

The third man, Lance Haslow, was perhaps around Tori's age—mid-forties. He struck Gina as one of those larger than life people. Tall, maybe six-two, big-boned and stocky, with a wide face. Thinning sandy hair. His shorts were loose, and his large feet were in flip-flops. His green T-shirt would be a double or triple X. He had a deep, booming voice and talked a lot, using big words. Clearly in love with the sound of his own voice.

Quite an eclectic group.

Gina had quickly seen how intent everyone was on winning. From the moment they'd boarded the boat in Perth at seven o'clock that morning they'd watched each other, assessing, calculating. They were six contestants chosen from over fifty thousand applicants. The sheer uniqueness of their group should bond them from the start. But what little they knew of the contest rules had produced just the opposite effect.

Gina turned back to the railing, wondering for the hundredth time what it would feel like to have a camera following her every move. How did these reality shows depict "reality" when people knew they were being filmed? She'd never liked the thought of it. Had almost dismissed that first advertising email about the opening of auditions. Especially when she thought about how heavy she'd look on TV. Wasn't the camera supposed to add ten pounds? As if her legs and thighs weren't big enough already. And her round face with extra fat beneath her chin would only look worse.

But then she'd read about the prize.

Their boat was nearing the island. Rocks framed either side of a small beach, the land beyond rising into thick green bushes and trees. The house was up high on a hill. Absolutely breathtaking. Who owned the place? Had Sensation Network, the new cable channel running *Dream Prize*, rented it from someone local? Aside from the house there was no other sign of civilization. Must be a privately owned island.

Just before they reached shore the captain turned the boat around and cut the engine, allowing the waves to back them toward the beach. As the stern brushed sand he dropped an anchor off the bow. When he was sure it held he let down a rear ladder and motioned for them to exit the boat.

Shari hesitated. "We're still in a foot of water."

"You'll dry." Aaron spoke dismissively. So much for being polite.

"Take your shoes off." Tori already carried her designer sandals.

Gina picked up her small purse. All their luggage had been collected early that morning. "So our suitcases are already here, right?"

The captain spread his arms. "This is all I know. Your bags are here, as promised. Follow the path up the hill to the house. Meet in the large ocean-view room. You'll receive further instructions there. I will return on Tuesday around four-thirty in the afternoon to pick you up. Have your bags ready."

Tuesday afternoon. It seemed so soon.

Gina searched the island. "Where's the camera crew and whoever else is needed to do the show? You'd think they'd be taping our arrival."

Aaron shrugged. "Must be inside."

Gina nodded. But uneasiness trickled through her veins. Everything about this had been so secretive. No one back home other than Ben knew she was on the show. And he didn't know *where* she was. Gina hadn't even known where she was flying to until she'd reached the airport. She'd been told only to "pack for a tropical climate." As for their cellphones and computers, all had been collected at their mainland hotel by their bus driver before they left for the boat. Like the captain, the bus driver knew only what little he'd been told.

Craig was looking around with an amazed smile. "Only three days here? I could stay forever."

"Ditto." Lance chuckled. He turned to the captain. "Thanks for the ride."

A shrug. "Okay, now go. You're supposed to be up there by nine o'clock. That's in ten minutes."

They did as they were told, Tori taking the lead. Gina rolled up her flowing beach pants. She held on to her shoes and descended the ladder, her wet feet collecting sand as she crossed the beach. The uphill path through green vegetation was well trod, not too hard on her bare feet. But it left her breathless. After a few minutes they reached a clearing around the house—and faced a gate in a wooden fence about four feet high.

"What have we here, ladies and gentlemen?" Lance touched the fence. It apparently circled the house. "Didn't see this from the beach."

"Me either." Tori glanced right and left. "Seems out of place. What's to keep out? Besides, it's not very high."

"Maybe the owner has a small dog," Shari said.

Aaron undid the latch and swung the gate open. It creaked. He ushered everyone through and closed it.

The cleared area around the house couldn't be more than thirty feet—most of it again going uphill. Stone steps were cut into that hill. Gina mounted them up to where the house stood, then gazed back over the top of the vegetation toward the ocean. The boat was already fading into the horizon. It was a done deal now, no turning back.

Still, with the camera crew, they'd have help in case of any emergency.

The group stood near the left corner of the porch. This close, Gina could see the house needed a paint job. Nothing terrible. But certainly not the fresh look she'd expect, given it would be filmed for millions of viewers.

She beat back another wave of unease and followed the rest across the porch, still carrying her sandals.

The downstairs glass turned out to be six sliding doors. Between each door were high wooden walls that jutted out about five feet onto the deck, affording a semi-private area just outside each door. At each room the curtains were closed. Gina tried the first door she came to. Locked. The second and third were also.

"Looks like a boutique hotel set-up," she said. "Bedrooms all in a row, one for each of us."

So—where was the film crew staying?

"The ocean view room must be upstairs." Tori moved past Gina.

"The film crew's not exactly waving us in, are they." Craig headed for a circular staircase at the far end of the deck.

In a line, they mounted the narrow curving steps. The second floor deck was spectacular. It had a roof to keep out the beating sun, a wood floor, scattered tables and chairs, and a sweeping view of the ocean.

"What a glorious abode." Lance spread his beefy arms.

Sure was. But Gina felt a pull to get inside the house and meet whoever was waiting for them. She hurried over to investigate a sliding door in the center of the deck. Unlocked. "Here!"

She stepped inside to a huge great room with more wooden flooring and various conversation areas of couches and chairs. Ceiling fans and lots of large windows. Décor in a soft teal and off white. A large round clock with gold spikes all around its face, like sun rays, hung on the back wall. All looked normal for a vacation home.

Except for the center of the room. There stood a round pedestal table. On the table, facing them, sat a monitor, its wires disappearing into a small hole cut in the floor. No computer. No keyboard. Just the screen, ringed by six identical leather-covered notebooks lying on the table. One black Sharpie sat by the monitor.

The room was stuffy and hot, as if it had been closed up for some time. It was also empty of people.

"Hello?" Craig called.

Silence.

The six contestants looked at each other.

Aaron headed toward the central table, his face expressionless. Gina followed, shoving her sunglasses up on her head.

"We need to open the windows." Tori fanned her face. "Get some air in here." She began her task, a breeze quickly easing the heat in the room.

Gina picked up a notebook. Nothing inside but blank paper and an attached pen held by a loop of fabric. Aaron examined a second notebook. Same thing. He put it down and focused on the monitor. Frowning, he leaned over and pushed the *on* button. The screen filled with the words *Dream Prize* in large letters against an ocean background.

"Ah, progress." Lance's resonant voice filled the room.

"Yeah." Craig came over and took hold of a notebook. "Just not what I was expecting. I figured we'd finally see someone face-to face. A host. A camera crew."

"Me too." That was an understatement. Gina shifted on her feet. The show's long audition process had all been done through email, video, and a final phone call with George Fry, the friendly and helpful producer. Of course she'd checked everything out along the way—the Sensation Network website, the show. Even had a lawyer look over the contract. But this just seemed ... off.

Aaron ran a finger along his jaw. "I don't think there's anyone else here."

The back of Gina's neck tingled. "There'd better be a phone or some way to communicate with the outside world. We've been left here alone for three days."

Shari shot her a look. "What you mean? We're gonna be filmed. Millions of people back home will be watching, starting tonight."

"I know but ... where's the crew? And the cameras? Where's someone to help immediately if we need it?"

Aaron was gazing at the far corner of the ceiling. "There." He pointed.

Everyone's head tipped that direction.

"And there." He indicated the other end of the room, then turned around. "Every corner's got a camera. Indicator lights are on. See the green? We're being recorded."

Gina sucked in a breath.

"Oh!" Shari took off her sunglasses and smiled at a camera like it was her oldest friend. Her eyes were a stunning deep green. "Hey, everyone. Didn't know you were there."

Well, now, nothing subtle about her playing to the audience. *And may it cost you points, Little Missy.*

Aaron glanced out the windows. "Probably cameras outside, too."

Craig tapped the notebook in his hand. "It's all beginning to make sense. The way we weren't told many details." He paused. "At least I wasn't."

"Me either." Lance shrugged. "But we were warned things would be secretive right up to the day of the show. All part of the purposeful media launch, right?"

Craig nodded. "That's what they told me. And I guess ... maybe the audience gets to watch us figure out what's going on from the beginning?"

"Or maybe they know more than we do." Shari stuck her sunglasses on her head. "The media blast for the show started after we left home. George Fry told me it would be everywhere—on Facebook and Twitter and Instagram. Plus, Sensation Network people will be on all the morning talk shows." She pointed a black nail at a camera, then posed her hand on her hip. "I'm thinking your plan, George Fry, was to get us out of the country first, so we couldn't hear what you're telling the audience." Shari's voice lilted.

Was this girl for real?

But she was probably right, Gina thought. Imagine the surprise of Gina's family and friends when they learned she was on this show in Australia. She'd told everyone she was leaving today for a vacation in Mexico with Ben.

Shari looked toward a doorway on the right, leading to a hallway. "Well then, I'm gonna go check the bedrooms and make sure my suitcases got here. And look for other cameras." She winked up toward the corner and headed for the door.

And good riddance. But not a good plan. Whatever happened next, Gina figured, would likely happen here.

"Remember what the captain said?" Lance raised his eyebrows. "That we were supposed to be up here in ten min—"

"Hey." Aaron pointed at the monitor.

The ocean scene and *Dream Prize* letters were fading. When it was gone a man appeared, sitting in a chair against a solid white background, his legs spread and hands interlaced. He had dark, thick hair and eyebrows, with a hard cut to his jaw.

The man gave a slight smile. "Welcome to *Dream Prize*."

Gina's breath stalled. *Here we go.* Anxiety and hope whirled through her. Forget the surprises, the secretive nature of the game to this point. What mattered now was winning.

For us, Ben. For the baby we long for with all our hearts.

Chapter 2

The man onscreen tapped his thumbs together. "I'm the producer, George Fry. I trust you all had a pleasant trip."

Craig Emberly felt his heart clutch. He'd been waiting for this moment for so long. All the planning, the gut-wrenching work it had taken to get here. Every contestant had come to win a dream prize. Too bad for the rest. He'd be the only winner.

He glanced at Shari, the dark-haired little babe who was just leaving the room. Her head jerked at the sound from the monitor. "Oh!" She trotted back to it, her sandals clacking against the floor. Her green eyes shone as she leaned toward the screen.

George Fry inclined his head. "As you know you've been selected out of over fifty thousand applications from around the country. So a quick pat on the back to each of you for getting this far. But of course, this is just the beginning. You, and all viewers along with you, are about to embark on a journey such has never been seen before in a reality show. A twisting, tangled challenge of collecting information about each other.

"Last night as you slept the media blitz, costing millions of dollars, was launched. Viewers in the U.S. and many other countries are now hearing about the 'Reality

Show of the Century.' They've had just enough time to line up their machines for all the hours of recording. Viewers are watching you now. You may have noticed the cameras in the ceiling corners of the room. Cameras are also throughout the house and surrounding the property. These are state of the art technology, using digital filming capabilities to record anytime day or night. The cameras are motioned-sensored, turning on when someone enters a room. The video feed is continually sent over our satellite-based Wi-Fi to our production studio in the U.S. In our studio are technicians who can control any camera when it clicks on, such as for zooming in and out. Audio pick-up is very sensitive. Whisper, and we will hear you.

"The only rooms in which cameras are not set to record are in the bedrooms. Your bedroom is a place for each of you to get away when you need to. And believe me, you *will* need to."

"Told ya about the media advertising," Shari whispered.

"Shh!" Tori flapped her hand—Blondie, the well dressed one. She was a take-charge female, lacking no confidence and taking no prisoners.

"By the way, each of you should enjoy your bedroom. It's been decorated just for you." Fry smiled.

"Now I'm going to tell you how the show works, including all the rules. Listen carefully. This is the only time you'll hear them."

Aaron—the Chinese guy of few words—snatched a notebook off the table. Craig still held onto his. He opened it and pulled out the pen. His fingers trembled, which ticked him off. No reason to not be totally in control of himself here.

The other five contestants dangled pens over paper, too, ready to write.

George Fry held up a finger. "One. As mentioned, the cameras follow you everywhere. *Unless* you are in your bedroom, you are being filmed. Without camera crews in your face, you will be able to act more naturally. As film from each camera rolls into our production studio, our team will be at work splicing all the feeds to present the show in as real time as possible. Which means *Dream Prize* will run on our new Sensation Network channel twenty-four hours a day."

Craig ogled the monitor.

"See why we call it the Reality Show of the Century?" George Fry spread his hands. "No hours of taping left on the cutting room floor. *Everything* you say and do will be viewable. At night while you all sleep, the feeds from various cameras will have a chance to catch up to real time. And at the bottom of their TV screens viewers will constantly be told what hour, Australian time, is currently running."

George Fry paused, as if to allow the information to sink in. "No other network has launched in such a remarkable way. Regardless of who wins this battle, all six of you will go down in history as the contestants in the show that forever changed television."

Shari smiled. Wasn't she just sizzling with confidence.

"Before we move on—one more thing about the cameras. Each of you will see a camera and a monitor in your bedroom. But that camera is not running and will never run unless you turn it on. If you want to talk straight to the viewers one-on-one, without other contestants hearing, this is the way to do it. Maybe you'll want to go over your notes and clues—what you suspect you've uncovered so far. Maybe you'll want to tell viewers more about yourselves. I encourage you to do this. It will give them a chance to hear your private thoughts. After all, you want them to like you. And their opinions could change hour to hour. Each viewer will be allowed twelve votes per day per device."

"One-on-one time. I applaud." Big guy Lance made a circle on his paper.

The man had talked nearly the whole boat ride over, and in silvery phrases. Sounding oh so educated and cultured.

"Second"—Fry held up two fingers—"the game is won by earning the most points. You earn a point for every viewer vote. At the end, the person who comes closest to solving the riddle of the game will triple his or her points—likely making that person the winner.

"A set of clues will be given on this monitor today and tomorrow at nine in the morning and five in the afternoon. In addition, at two o'clock and eight o'clock this monitor will announce which of you received the most votes in that time period. That person will be entitled to an extra clue about the contestant of his or her choice. If you are the winner, turn on the camera in your bedroom and name that contestant and your question. You will be given instructions on your personal monitor regarding how to receive the answer."

Craig was taking notes furiously.

"The last day—Tuesday—has a more intensified schedule. Clues at nine and two o'clock. *One* announcement of the most votes winner at noon. There will be no second winner announcement, although viewers can continue voting until three o'clock."

Fry paused.

"Now. You can also *lose* points. There are two ways this can happen. One is being caught in a lie. The other is going outside the fenced area. In both cases you will lose half of all points earned that day." Fry smiled. "Of course you will be tempted to lie to each other. All the better to throw others off the course of learning the truth about yourself. So lie if you want. Just know you're taking a chance. If a clue is released that proves you lied—you'll lose points. This will happen quietly. You will not be notified.

"You can also lose points by going over the fence to the east, south, or north. This is because you would be outside the range of cameras. You are permitted to go through the west gate and down to the beach. Cameras will pick up your movements on the beach, but not your words. Perhaps not the best way to earn viewer votes."

"You're kidding me." Shari made a sound in her throat. "We're on an island—and we can't spend time on the *beach*?"

She'd probably brought a bunch of bikinis to show off her body. *Too bad for you, chickie.*

"There is one action," Fry continued, "that will result in immediate disqualification from the show. That is harming or trying to disable any camera."

Fry raised his chin. "Now, how does the show end? At four o'clock Tuesday afternoon, two hours after you've received the last set of clues, you all will gather before this monitor to hear the winner's name announced. At any time up until three o'clock you can turn on your bedroom camera, say 'I am ready to solve the game' and state your conclusion about each contestant. Once you do that, once you say those words, your answer is locked in. If more than one person has the same number of correct answers, then the first to record those answers will be awarded the triple points. Have your bags packed before the winner announcement. You will leave immediately afterwards."

Fry pointed toward them. "Not only does one of you win—so do some lucky and astute viewers out there. The first viewer to log into our game's website and record all the right answers will win one million dollars. The second will win half a million. And the third will receive one hundred thousand. But, viewers, take your time to be sure. You can only record your answers once. Like the contestants, you have until three o'clock on Tuesday to record your answers. Winning viewers' names will be posted on our website immediately following the end of the show."

George Fry shifted in his chair. "I have thrown a lot of information at you. You may find this recap of the schedule helpful."

Fry faded from the screen, and text appeared.

Sunday and Monday

9 a.m. and 5 p.m.—list of clues
2 p.m. and 8 p.m.—winner of most votes announcement

Tuesday

9 a.m. and 2 p.m.—list of clues
12 noon—winner of most votes announcement
3 p.m.—deadline for locking in your answers
4 p.m.—*Dream Prize* winner announced

Fry reappeared on the monitor. He leaned forward, palms on his thighs. "And now—the most important part. *What* are you six contestants supposed to guess about each other?" His tone edged. "Certainly not mere places of residence and occupations. Where's the excitement in that? In fact, I'm about to give you that information to start. And as much as you may want to know what each person has chosen as his or her dream prize, that's not your main agenda either.

"So what is *Dream Prize* all about?" Fry straightened. One corner of his mouth curled. "What you want to discover is the *worst* about each other."

Shari sucked in air. Craig froze.

"Take note of this list," Fry said. Again, he faded from the monitor and text appeared, written on a scroll:

The Seven Deadly Sins

Lust: intense and uncontrolled sexual desire

Gluttony: overindulgence and over-consumption of anything to the point of waste

Sloth: apathy, idleness, and wastefulness of time

Wrath: unrighteous feelings of hatred and anger

Envy: jealousy and resentment of the possessions or accomplishments of others

Pride: excessive love and admiration of oneself, leading to contempt of others

"What *is* this?" Tori sounded disgusted.

"I don't know." Craig looked around. Gina, the big gal Hispanic, gaped at the monitor, round-eyed.

"Oh, please." Shari seemed to have recovered. She flipped her hand in the air.

Aaron and Lance were writing, their faces tight. Craig started jotting down the words.

The list faded. George Fry reappeared.

"So why are these seven sins listed?" Fry raised an eyebrow. "Because each of you represents one of them. It is your job to determine *who* is *which*, including yourself."

"*What?*" Gina's mouth hung open.

The air in the room shifted. Aaron's eyes narrowed. Shari's head drew back. Lance stilled. They all exchanged glances, the expressions on their faces shuttering.

"Now there are a few twists, of course. Makes things more interesting." Fry smiled again—and it wasn't friendly. "There are only six of you, which means one sin isn't represented. Second, one of you *may* not represent any sin. *If* that's the case, then only five are represented. But that may not be the case. You decide."

Fry cupped his chin. His eyes seemed to grow darker, and his tone hardened. "You see, each of you has a secret. A *damning* one. If you can discover someone's secret, you will be close to figuring out which sin that person represents. And, by the way, if you win the most votes in a time period and get to ask for an extra clue, you cannot ask for someone's secret to be revealed or what sin they represent. That would be far too easy. You *can* ask for additional information to help you discover that secret."

"Wait, that's not what this show is supposed to be about." Shari' voice turned whiny. "And *I* don't represent some sin anyway. Or have a secret."

Lance gave a booming but nervous laugh. "Neither do I. And even if I did harbor some 'secret,' I can assure you I wouldn't have put it on my application form."

"Me either." Craig gestured with his chin to Aaron. "Who would do that?"

Aaron shrugged.

On the monitor George Fry sat silently, as if allowing time for the unsettling news to sink in.

The contestants had filled out lengthy questionnaires, pages long. But a secret? Craig would never let *his* be revealed, that was for sure. He saw the inevitable question flit across Gina's round face — *how would they know?* As if she, too, had something to hide. She shook her head. "They're playing with us." She gazed at Craig, then at a camera, as if to say *Right?*

Tori looked like she'd been punched in the stomach. "I don't want to do this." Her chin rose. "I'm not here to be degraded by some kind of false, trumped-up story about me. And I sure don't care to be looking for the worst in other people."

"Right. Me too." Shari tossed her dark mane.

"Chill out." Aaron aimed them a disgusted look. "Keep listening."

"Yeah," Craig said. "Let's just calm down. Whatever 'secrets' he's talking about can't be anything major. Not if they just used what we wrote on the application form."

Tori locked eyes with him. Her expression read — *but what if it's more than that?* She firmed her mouth, then turned back to the monitor with a wary expression.

George Fry held up a hand. "All right. Now that you've had time to digest all that information, it's time for the basic data on each of you. You'll only hear this once. When I say your name, contestants, please raise your hand for the sake of viewers."

Fry paused again. The room around Craig reverberated with the sound of deep breaths, everyone intent on keeping calm. He kept himself still, poising his pen over a clean sheet of paper.

"Ready?" Fry continued. "The first contestant is Craig Emberly, age twenty-nine."

Craig held up his hand and nodded at the camera on his right.

"Craig lives in Malibu, California. He created and manages a foundation for the treatment of multiple sclerosis patients and further research of the disease."

Fry paused, giving them time to write down the information.

"Contestant two is Aaron Wang, age twenty-eight."

Chinese Guy Aaron raised his hand, his face expressionless.

"Aaron lives in Austin, Texas. He is a computer engineer for a large firm, working out of his home."

Another pause.

The oppressive feeling in the room lessened a little. This was normal stuff. Expected. Except maybe the ages.

"Contestant three is Lance Haslow, age forty-seven."

Big Guy Lance raised his arms and focused on a camera with a beefy smile. "Greetings. I only regret we can't meet in person."

"Lance lives in Sacramento, California. He is a local radio talk show host. His show focuses on community issues."

A radio guy. Wouldn't surprise anybody, with a voice like that. Craig wrote down the information.

"Contestant four is Tori Hattinger, age forty-five."

Take No Prisoners Tori raised a hand, cringing as her age was announced. The large blue stone on her fourth finger sparkled.

"She lives in Cupertino, California and is Vice President of a successful computer software business.

"Contestant Five is Shari Steele, age twenty-three."

Little Babe Shari had pulled herself together. She flashed another seductive smile toward the camera.

"She lives in Los Angeles, California. She is an actress."

Surprise, surprise.

"And contestant six is Gina Corrales, age thirty-nine."

Big Gal Gina barely raised her hand. She looked scared to death.

"She lives in Pasadena, California, and is a real estate agent.

"Now I'll give you a minute to finish your notes."

Lance looked up from his writing and caught Craig's eye. "Notice something weird? Five of us live in California."

Craig consulted his notes. "You're right. That's ... interesting."

"Now, good luck to all of you," George Fry said. "This is the last you will see of me until Tuesday. All information from here on out will be printed on the screen. It will remain there for five minutes, then will disappear, not to be repeated. So be on time and ready to write everything down. Viewers, once these clues are given to contestants, you'll be able to access them anytime on our *Dream Prize* website."

Fry raised an eyebrow. "By the way, contestants, one more thing." He smiled again—a sadistic expression. "Did I mention all the clues are about your secrets?"

All the oxygen sucked out of the room.

Aaron emitted a cold laugh. "What *is* this?"

"Hang on," Craig said. "Can't be that bad."

But all the other contestants now looked petrified, their faces barren and thoughts exposed. Even Shari the actress had lost her plastic smile. What if this show *had* dug into their personal lives and was now about to release clues about some dark secret they carried? Clues twice a day—for three days. On *national television?*

"He's just being dramatic." Lance's words boomed. "Makes for exciting viewing. I do the same thing on the radio."

Gina slid a sideways glance at Tori. Clearly she wanted to believe that.

"And now we begin—with the first list of clues." Fry chuckled, a hard, guttural sound. "You should find them *very interesting.*"

"Wait ..." Gina's face had lost its color.

Craig's heart rat-tatted in his chest. He glanced around again. All the others wore similar expressions. Guarded. Leary. *Guilty.* As if this show threatened to strip them bare.

They were stuck on this remote island, all of them. Trapped in this show. No way to stop whatever came next. No way at all.

George Fry disappeared from the screen, and the "Sunday 9 a.m." list of clues faded in.

DREAM PRIZE

Sunday 9 a.m.

On June 4, 2013, escrow closed for a couple buying a home in the Cheviot Hills neighborhood of Los Angeles. *Gina Corrales* was their real estate agent.

~~~

On March 3, 2013, *Craig Emberly's* niece, Sarah, was diagnosed with multiple sclerosis.

~~~

On January 7 and 8, 2014, *Aaron Wang* attended a computer software convention in Los Angeles.

~~~

On April 16, 2012, *Shari Steele* auditioned for a part in the new TV show *Last Bend*.

~~~

On March 13, 2012, *Lance Haslow* interviewed a man on his radio show who had overcome his drug addiction at a local rehab facility.

~~~

On December 19, 2001, *Tori Hattinger* failed to show up for her waitressing job in Nashville, Tennessee.

Chapter 3

Lance Haslow ran his eyes down the clues, looking for the one about himself. There. The penultimate one.

His breath snagged.

Wait a minute, wait a minute.

He read it again—and felt sweat pop out on his forehead.

First George Fry's taunting words. As if he'd caught them in his fist like mice and plotted to make them squirm in front of the world. Now this clue. Forget what Craig had hoped aloud—this *wasn't* something from Lance's application form. He had never given the show producers that information.

The clue mentioned a man he'd interviewed on his radio show. Who'd been cured—at least at the time—of his drug habit. That had to be Bruce Egan. No other possibilities.

Lance swallowed. This needed to stop. Now.

No one else was moving. Pens should have been furiously scribbling before the clues faded. But the other contestants seemed as frozen as Lance. He glanced at the business woman, Tori. Her face was pale.

Dead air.

The thought kicked through Lance's brain. Dead air—silence—was anathema to radio. One second to a listener could feel like ten. Ten seconds like forever. Lance repressed the desire to look at the cameras. Millions of viewers were watching right now—and here he stood, visibly shell-shocked.

Lance pressed his pen against the paper and forced himself to write. Shoving aside his fear, he concentrated on jotting down the clues. All of them seemed so innocuous. Boring, even. Not the kind of lead information he'd choose for a topic on his radio show. After all, he was Mr. Sacramento, garrulous and entertaining. Presenting the "Untold Story" from the community five days a week during the peak commuter hour of five to six in the afternoon.

But to anyone else, the clue about him would seem innocuous as well.

Somehow as he wrote, Lance forced his breathing to steady. For a minute the only sound in the room was the scratch of pen against paper. The instincts of the other contestants had kicked in.

Clues written down, Lance checked his work. It would be too easy with his reeling mind to make a mistake in a date or place. And something told him every detail mattered.

Satisfied, he smacked his notebook shut with one large hand. Forced a smile and took a step backward. He started to look around the room, feigning further nonchalance, but his eyes drew back to the monitor. What if something else materialized?

Lance focused on the screen, memorizing the clues, until it faded to black.

Other notebooks slowly closed.

The tension in the room gelled.

Lance was adroit at pulling out someone else's story, particularly when met with circumlocution. That was his job, and the very reason he'd felt so confident he could win this show. Now he would need those skills more than ever. All he sensed from the other contestants was distancing and self defense. A proper response. For *Dream Prize* was not focused on merely learning facts about each other, as he'd assumed. It was about judging.

Bruce Egan.

This couldn't be what Lance thought it was. It made no sense. Everything would still be fine. Just an unsettling coincidence. The interview with Bruce was hardly secret in itself. Anyone could delve into the online archives of "Untold Story" and listen to past interviews. Besides, George Fry could not have possibly uncovered Lance's secret. No one knew that except two other people—and they both had strong reason for diligent silence.

As for the infamous Seven Deadly Sins, none of them applied to Lance. He was a good man, a good father to his son. He'd always strived to give Scott the best, especially after Lance and Scott's mother had divorced years ago. Now that Scott was a young man—twenty-two—they were more than parent and child. They were compadres. What Lance had done, he'd been forced to do. Who would turn his back on his own son?

Lance studied the other contestants. Who was Envy? Pride? Greed?

He caught Gina's eye. Her cheeks had gone from pale to over-pink, her smile tremulous. Aaron was surveying her, his face stern. Tori had sunk into a chair and was staring at the floor. Craig's back was ramrod straight. Only Shari feigned unconcern. After all she was an actress. But her smile was too fixed, too tight.

She lifted her shoulders. "What fun this is going to be!"

Indeed.

She tucked her notebook under her arm. "Now I'm gonna go explore the house."

Good riddance.

Lance knew her type. They made the worst kind of radio interviewees. Never real, never truly personal. They said only what they thought listeners wanted to hear, shared only "from their hearts" what would make them sound their best. Plastic, that's what they were. Shari Steele lived off her looks, parading her pulchritude at every turn.

But right now she was clearly as rattled as Lance. How long before that persona cracked?

That might be entertaining to watch.

Lance focused on his notebook again, reading over the clues. They all meant something, undoubtedly. Nothing innocuous here.

The room was so hot. Lance headed outside to the long deck and leaned against the railing, his notebook dropped at his feet. The ocean breeze ruffled over his face. If only it could unruffle his soul.

He sensed movement beside him and glanced over to see Craig at the railing about six feet away, still holding on to his notebook. He was looking out over the water, squinting against the glare.

Lance ran the clue about Craig through his mind — the man's niece being diagnosed with MS. How could that implicate Craig in some dark deed? No one caused a person to have MS.

So which of the Seven Deadly Sins was he? Wrath? Sloth? Maybe Lust. Maybe the man was heavy into pornography and would sleep with all three women before the show was over. Maybe he'd molested his niece.

Lance winced. What a heinous thought.

He cleared his throat. "Sorry to hear your niece has MS. Sarah, right?"

Craig gave a little nod. "Yeah."

"How old is she?"

A second's hesitation. "Fourteen."

Fourteen. That would mean she was nine when diagnosed. Lance couldn't imagine experiencing such an illness with his son.

But then they'd had their own nightmare.

"Is she ... I mean, how bad are her symptoms?"

Craig tapped the wooden railing. "She's in a wheelchair. Sweetest thing. Always thinking about other people."

Lance heard faint voices in the great room behind him. Sounded like Tori and Gina.

"Is that why you started your foundation for MS?"

Craig was, what—twenty-nine? Which meant he was twenty-four when he'd created the foundation. Such entities required a plethora of dollars. How had he acquired it at that young age?

Craig's smile was sad. "Yeah." He put down his notebook and pulled a wallet from his back shorts pocket. Took out a picture and handed it to Lance. "Here."

Lance studied the photo of a young blonde teenager in a wheelchair, her arms spread and a huge grin on her face. Her entire expression beamed. Lance's heart panged. He handed the picture back to Craig.

"She's beautiful. What's the occasion?"

Craig slid the photo back into his wallet. "No special day. Annie's just always like that." He slipped the wallet into his pocket. "In a wheelchair, but so vibrant."

Lance nodded. Some people possessed that ability, no matter their situation in life. "Your foundation must aid a lot of people."

"It does." Craig sounded sure of himself. "We're going to eradicate the disease. Don't know when. But we will."

"I hope you do. Is that your Dream Prize? Getting ten million for more research?"

Craig straightened, a veil falling over his expression, as if he realized he'd said too much. He picked up his notebook and returned to the house.

Lance contemplated the exchange. The wind swirled over him, drying the sweat on his forehead. He lifted his face to the sun and closed his eyes. Took a couple deep breaths. He must remain calm. Focus. Better to concentrate on solving the mysteries of the other contestants than on his own simmering fears. He picked up his notebook and jotted down what he'd learned about Craig.

But Lance's mind soon returned to his own clue. *Bruce Egan*. Why him, out of the thousands of people Lance had interviewed over the years?

A horrifying thought scuttled through Lance's brain. What if the next three days descended from the heady pursuit of victory to the desperation of saving himself—and his son—from prison?

Chapter 4

"Now this is a kitchen."

Shari Steele stood at the entrance to the room, taking in the long granite island, the white cabinets and huge sink. Her purse hung off one shoulder, sunglasses on her head. She held her notebook with her left hand, leaning against the threshold, her hip stuck out a little. She'd practiced the pose at home for the cameras, getting it just right until it showed her figure at its best. Beautiful and cool and calm—that's how she wanted to look.

Especially now. Because inside she felt like Jello.

That clue about herself! *Why* did they say that? She hadn't mentioned anything on her application form about auditioning for *Last Bend*. Somebody at the Sensation Network had done some digging, right down to the date.

But it couldn't mean anything. Right? Okay, she'd freaked out at first, but she had to believe everything would be fine. That producer, George Fry—who'd tried to be all Freddy Krueger creepy—probably knew the producer of *Last Bend*. So they'd compared notes, that's all. Now Shari had to make up for the fact that she'd looked scared to death after that clue.

She could not let her guard down like that again. Especially now that she knew how important viewer votes would be. She should have it made in spades. What other contestant would talk to viewers so easily? And her Dream Prize fit perfectly with all this. Shari wanted the lead in a major motion picture—the big break she'd dreamed of for so long. Worked *hard* for. Imagine not only landing the role, but also all the free publicity from this show leading up to the film's release. She'd be a star before she was a star! Her career would be made.

"One day you'll go back to California and follow your dream," her mom had said. And that's exactly what Shari had done.

She let her gaze roam over the kitchen ceiling. In the right far corner sat a camera. And in the left one. She turned around. Yup. One in each of those corners, too.

Shari smiled at the camera on her left. "Wish you all could be here with me, just to feel the ocean air. Although it's kinda stuffy in this room." She put down her notebook and busied herself with opening the windows. On the far right stood a sliding glass door leading out to a wooden deck. She pushed back the door as far as she could.

Then she stood in the middle of the kitchen, hands on her hips. "Ah, love that breeze!"

She closed her eyes, feeling the millions of people watching her.

"I know, let's check out the refrigerator!" She pulled back the large door and let out a little squeal. "Look! The thing's like totally full. Can you see it?" She opened the door wider, pointing at the camera that would cover the area where she stood. "All kinds of drinks, and wine, and cheese, and stuff." She investigated the drawers, pulling out vegetables and meats, and naming them for the camera. "I don't know if we're all supposed to make meals together, or just do it on our own. I don't eat meat, myself. And I stick to fresh veggies and fruit as much as possible. And I love to juice. Which reminds me ..." She closed the refrigerator door and looked around the counters. "Oh, good, there it is! A blender."

Shari heard footsteps approaching. She turned her head, listening.

"I think someone's coming," she whispered to the camera, raising her shoulders conspiratorially. "Let's go on downstairs to the bedrooms. See which one is mine."

Before she could leave the kitchen, Aaron appeared in the doorway. The long, lean Chinese. Hair cut short. Kind of deep-set eyes. All in all not bad looking. If he wasn't so wooden.

Shari flashed him a smile. "Oh. Hi."

"Hello."

Aaron stood straight and contained. Only his head and eyes moved as he surveyed the kitchen and the cameras. "Good." His face remained expressionless.

Wow. How would viewers take to *him*? He sure wasn't going out of his way to relate. And when he talked, it was like in syllables. *"Me Tarzan, you Jane."*

Well, me Shari, you Aaron, and I'm going to wipe the floor with you.

"Yeah it is good. And there's lots of food. In the refrigerator, anyway. I haven't even looked in the pantry yet, but I bet it's loaded."

Aaron nodded, then walked to the refrigerator to check it out.

"Do you like to cook?" Shari asked.

"No." Aaron opened the vegetable drawer.

"Does your wife? Or live-in girlfriend?"

"I live alone."

"Oh. Well, what do you eat, then?"

Aaron closed the fridge door. "Didn't say I don't cook. I just don't like it. I make what I need to eat."

Aaron's face never changed. This guy was a computer nerd, right? Worked at home? Yeah, it fit. Definitely not a lot of personality going on here.

How original.

"And you?" Aaron folded his arms.

"What?"

"You don't look like the type to cook or clean."

"Well, I —"

"Bet your room's a mess."

Shari bristled. "For your information I haven't even *been* to my room yet."

"I meant in general. Where you live."

Well, good guess for him. So he was smarter than he looked. Shari had her own guess. This guy was Pride. See how he gazed down his nose at her?

She tilted her head and gave the man her best huffy look. "What makes you think you know so much about people?"

"I don't. I know computers. They're predictable."

Was that a hint of sadness flitting across his face?

Shari softened her expression. "I'm sorry."

"About what?"

"That someone hurt you."

He drew back his head and stiffened. "I never said that."

"You didn't have —"

"Stop." He pointed at her. "Stop right now."

He strode from the kitchen.

Shari listened to him go, then mugged at a camera, her eyes widening. "Well. Wonder what *that* was all about."

Chapter 5

Aaron Wang pounded down the hardwood stairs to the lower floor, simmering. Shari Steele. What a princess. Had to be Pride. Prancing around like she was the world's greatest gift. How dare she pretend to know him? Say that in front of the viewers?

He was already uneasy enough.

This show—things weren't right. He wanted to leave, and now. That clue about his attending the software convention in L.A. two years ago—*where* did they get that? And why?

It could not be what it looked like.

Aaron hit the landing and slowed, pulling the pen from his notebook. He had to stop this mind rant. Keep on task. Everything he learned must be recorded. He was a computer programmer. Precise. Detailed. Logical.

He would win this.

Shari—fake, he wrote. *Acts compassionate to pull out info.*

Aaron replaced the pen and leaned against the wall. The stairway was at one end of the house, ending near a back door. He walked away from the door and turned right, gazing down a long, wide hall. There were windows on the right, looking to the backyard. Six doors on the left. Bedrooms.

Which one was his?

He checked door one. No name on it. He knocked.

Silence.

Aaron opened the door and stepped inside to a stuffy room. The far wall was mostly curtains. Closed.

The room was gold and white. Laced fluffy bedspread. Two suitcases on the bed. On top of one—a key labeled "Room 1." Name on the luggage tags—Tori Hattinger. Gold area rug on a wooden floor. Near the curtains in one corner, a white armchair with fuzzy blanket and pillow. At the other corner, a tall dresser with four drawers.

Three photographic prints on the walls. On the left wall by the side of the bed, the words "President and CEO" in calligraphy letters. By the curtains, a building labeled Vanderbilt Medical School. To the right above the desk, the blurred image of an ambulance with flashing lights.

Cozy photo.

Executive style desk and leather rolling chair. On the wall by the desk, close to the ambulance picture hung a camera. Monitor on the desk. And a plaque that read *Serros*.

Serros. A big computer software company in Silicon Valley. Where Tori Hattinger worked?

What did George Fry say? *You'll enjoy your room—it's been decorated just for you.*

Aaron pulled out his pen. There were clues here. Probably in the other rooms, too. How many could he get to before they were claimed? Quickly, he wrote in his notebook.

When he was done, he checked the closed door on the same side of the room as the desk. It opened to a bathroom with a clothes closet.

Aaron left the bedroom and moved to the next.

The layout of the second room was the same but flipped. And his suitcases were on the bed. Black and beige colors. Plain desk and chair a lot like he had in his home.

Too much like it.

Not cool.

On the desk — a piece of stationery from the company where he worked. On the wall by the bed — a photo of a yacht on the ocean. Aaron's heart surged. Of course. His dream prize was a yacht and crew to sail the world, taking Lisa, the woman he'd loved since college. The woman who only saw him as a friend. Who'd married someone else, a man who ended up beating and abusing her. Now she was divorced. Now she could be Aaron's. The yacht was actually *her* dream. With it, and the trip Aaron would offer her, he'd finally make Lisa love him.

Aaron pulled back the closed curtains. Saw a sliding glass door. Beyond it, his framed-in private area on the outside deck. Sweeping view of the tops of trees and the ocean.

He let the curtains fall shut and noticed the nearby picture — a rugged snowy mountain in China. A shiver shook him. How did they know this? His father's name was Shan, meaning mountain. Shan was raised in China — in a house with of a view of that peak.

Aaron raked his eyes away. Turned to study the photo above his desk. An outside shot of a Los Angeles restaurant. *The* restaurant. Where he'd heard the news.

"Each of you has a secret ..."

His notebook slipped to the floor.

Aaron stared at the picture, veins sizzling. Seconds ticked by.

He snapped himself out of it. *Move! Get to the other rooms while you can!*

Aaron snatched up his notebook. Grabbed his key from the bed and fled the room. Locked its door, stuffed the key in his pocket.

In the hall he stopped to listen. No one nearby.

He knocked on door three. No answer. He entered the room, decorated in blue and white. Started writing. Robot-like, fears shoved aside.

Room 3 photos bed to sliding door to desk —movie theater marquee, hospital room, Shari and beautiful friend. (Looks familiar.) On desk —brochure, Sundowner Apartments.

No time to figure what it all meant. No way would he let Shari catch him snooping. She'd throw a fit.

He left the room and went to door four. It was empty.

Lance Haslow's suitcases on the bed. Beige and brown colors. On the desk, a name holder with engraved letters *KXOY*. Aaron wrote it down. *Room 4 photos: beach and sunbathers. Lance and young boy. A courtroom.*

These photos—they all had to mean something. Something important. He'd sort it all out as soon as he could.

Aaron returned to the hall. No one around. His heart rattled. Two more to go.

Next room—Gina Corrales. Red and gold colors. *Room 5 photos —Baby. Wedding picture—Gina and husband. Real estate SOLD sign. Desk —coffee mug from Heights Realty.*

Almost done.

Aaron moved to room six. Knocked.

"Yes?"

He froze.

The door opened a crack. Craig peered out. "Need something?"

"Oh. No. I … was just looking for my room."

Craig eyed Aaron suspiciously. Why start at the far end of the hall? "Try again."

The door shut.

Aaron stepped back and pulled in deep breaths. He returned to his room and locked the door. Tossed his notebook on the desk and pulled his suitcases from the bed to the floor.

Should he open his curtains and sliding door, let some air in? The room was hot. But what if someone walked across the deck outside, beyond his side walls? They could come right into his private sitting area, peek in the room, see his pictures.

Not acceptable.

Three days in this room with that view—and he couldn't even enjoy it.

Aaron unlocked the sliding door and pushed it open but left the curtains closed. Maybe a little fresh air would filter inside.

He collapsed on his bed and pored over his notes, mind spinning. How to interpret what he'd seen in the bedrooms?

Three pictures in each one. And something on each desk. Did everything match the meaning of the items in his own room? If so …

First, the desk. On his own lay a piece of stationery from the company where he worked. Therefore: desk equaled something about the person's employment.

But Shari's desk held an apartment brochure. She couldn't work there. She was an actress.

Shari—brochure—why? he wrote in his notebook.

Second, the photos by each bed. Aaron turned his head to gaze at his yacht picture.

Lisa, there, at the bow. Me, beside her …

The bed picture represented the person's dream prize.

Third, the photo by the sliding door. Aaron focused on his picture of the cold Chinese mountain. His jaw flexed.

The door picture equaled something or someone influential in the person's life.

Fourth, the picture over each desk. Aaron stared at the photo over his own, the one of the restaurant.

The restaurant. That awful night.

The desk pictures represented some bad occurrence in the contestant's life.

Did they also connect to the person's secret?

Cold fear surged through Aaron. He jumped up and grabbed the picture from the wall. Shoved it under his bed. Then yanked down the photo of the mountain and pushed it under, too.

He stood in the middle of the room, breathing hard.

What he was imagining could not be possible. Nobody knew what he'd done. Nobody.

Then why were those photos here?

Aaron had gone to that restaurant only once in his life. He didn't even live in Los Angeles.

Wait.

The first set of clues. The one for Gina Corrales had been about her real estate clients buying a house in the Cheviot neighborhood of Los Angeles. Aaron had been struck by that.

He yanked his notebook off the desk. Skimmed over the clue. That house had been bought in June 2013.

Aaron's head came up. *June 2013.* Perfect timing.

Something slithered through his stomach.

Aaron flicked to the notes from Gina's room. The photo above her desk—the one representing a bad occurrence—was a real estate *sold* sign.

Aaron sat down hard on the bed, staring at his own writing.

Chapter 6

When no one answered her knock, Tori Hattinger eased open the door to the bedroom closest to the stairs and peeked inside. Her suitcases lay on the bed.

Finally—something easy.

She slipped inside and closed the door. Leaned against it. Here, she was out of the realm of cameras. For a moment she just stood there and breathed.

Her ankles were shaking.

Tori opened her eyes and looked over her room. The décor was beautiful. Gold and white, with a soft, comfy feel. Similar to what she'd have chosen herself.

But how could they know that?

The room was hot, and Tori was already sweating enough. She hurried over to open the curtains and sliding glass door. Immediate cooling air filtered inside, along with the swishing sound of leaves in the wind. The breeze, the ambiance, her little private deck area, the ocean view—all should be soothing. But it only unnerved her more, reminding her that she was trapped on an island with five strangers, and the world was watching.

What had she been thinking to come on this show?

Tori's gaze wandered to the wall above the desk — and her lungs went cold.

Hanging there was a framed photo of a speeding ambulance, lights flashing.

No.

That first clue about her missing work at the restaurant all those years ago had nearly knocked her over. Now this.

"That's not funny." She spoke the words aloud. They rang in her ears. It was the same tone she took at work when chewing out some employee who'd failed to carry out a task. And somehow that familiar tone helped Tori rally herself. After all, she wasn't some pawn who could be played. She was a business woman who'd worked her way up from nothing. The current vice president of Serros, and would-be president and CEO if she won this contest. How George Fry would finagle that, she didn't know and didn't care. She only knew he'd promised they could give her whatever dream prize she chose — and quickly. In fact, Fry had seemed intrigued at the challenge of providing her prize. Tori would rise to the head of Serros. And she would take it to heights that the current incompetent president and CEO would never accomplish. Tori Hattinger would turn Serros into a Fortune 500 company.

Mouth set, she examined the rest of her room. Next to the ambulance photo hung the camera George Fry had told them about. As if she'd ever want to turn that thing on in the only private space around.

Wait. It wasn't running. Correct?

She walked to it, placing her hand over the lens, just in case. She peered around the sides of the camera, finding a button. Pushed it. A green light came on. She smacked it again. The light went off.

Arms folded, Tori stood back and eyed the camera, still suspicious.

She headed into the bathroom and grabbed a hand towel off its rack. Folded it in half and hung it from the camera, covering the lens.

There.

Wait. George Fry had said a contestant would be disqualified for harming or disabling a camera. Was this considered disabling? Tori stared at the covered lens. She hadn't hurt the thing. And it didn't look like it was on anyway. Still ...

She heaved a sigh and snatched the towel away. Tossed it on the floor near the entrance to the bathroom.

Tori ran a hand through her hair, trying to refocus. After a moment she continued her examination of the room.

The monitor on her desk was small but adequate. The Serros plaque was nice. But where had they gotten it?

The graphic above her bed reading "President and CEO" was another apropos touch.

Tori's gaze landed on the photo by the sliding door. A Vanderbilt Medical School building.

She drew in another long breath.

One more thing she'd never mentioned on her application form. One more indication someone had dug deep into her past.

Why?

Tori half collapsed in the leather chair before her desk. The why was obvious, and no use denying it. George Fry had tricked her. Tricked all the contestants. No wonder he'd billed *Dream Prize* as "the show of the century." Who wouldn't watch it, given the promise to expose the contestants' secrets on live TV? Even viewers shocked at what was happening on the island would be riveted by the slow train wreck of six people's lives.

Unless she could stop it.

Tori fixed her eyes on the wood grain of the desk, deep in thought.

Of course she would be very careful regarding what she told the other contestants about herself. Maybe no one would be able to guess much. But the clues were the unknown factor. What if, all six combined, they presented the whole picture of that time in her life she so wanted to hide?

Tori frowned. This puzzle didn't make sense. That time in her life wasn't something she'd done wrong. In fact, she'd *been* wronged. All she'd done was manage to rise above it, turn the tables to meet her own needs. So how could it lead people to some major "deadly sin" she supposedly represented? The idea was crazy.

Clearly, she was the one who represented no sin at all.

Still, if her secret was revealed, it would shine light on the one weakness that could cast serious doubt about her ability to lead a company.

"Is that what's going on here, George Fry?" Tori leaned back and addressed the ceiling. "You want to destroy all of us sufficiently so that even the person who wins will never claim the prize? Because that person's very secret will make the prize unattainable."

Tori placed an elbow on the desk and rested her forehead against her palm. Had she ruined her life by coming here?

Some time later she straightened, glancing at her watch. Nearly ten-thirty. She needed to unpack. Freshen up. Pull her thoughts together. After that she'd go make some lunch.

At two o'clock the first winner of viewer votes would be announced, which would lead to that person receiving an extra clue. That winner wasn't going to be Tori if she kept hiding out in this room.

She mulled that over—and stayed where she was.
At five o'clock the next set of clues would appear.
Then repeat—for two more days.
Dread trickled through Tori's veins.

Chapter 7

In her room, Gina opened her curtains and sliding door. An immediate breeze washed over her. Thank goodness. She was so hot. She gazed at the ocean view, barely seeing it.

Her legs were weak.

The room was nice, although it could have been bigger. But the pictures on the walls had stopped Gina in her tracks.

She sat down next to the suitcases on her bed and stared at the photo above her desk. The print of a real estate *sold* sign.

It should mean nothing. She was a realtor, and realtors sold houses. But—first that clue about her clients buying the house in Cheviot Hills. Now this picture. During Gina's career, she'd led buyers to a house in the Cheviot neighborhood of Los Angeles only once. *The* house. At that time the selling realtor of that house had just printed new *sold* signs. Those signs were quickly replaced because the diva owner of that real estate agency decided she didn't like the new logo.

The photo above Gina's desk was a picture of that short-lived sign.

What was happening? What were the producers of this show trying to do to her? Was it all lies, everything they'd told her? Gina shifted to look at the wedding photo of her and Ben, then twisted around to view the picture by her bed—of a baby. Did these people want to wreck her marriage? Make it so she and Ben would never have a baby?

Could this game be that *sick*?

And how had they gotten her wedding picture in the first place?

Tears stung Gina's eyes. She wiped them away. She couldn't be thinking about this right. Everything had to have a normal explanation.

She straightened and gazed at the camera mounted on the wall above her desk. If she turned it on, it couldn't possibly film the *sold* sign picture beside it. But it would certainly take in the baby photo. And maybe even her and Ben's wedding picture near the door.

Well, she could just do something about that.

Gina removed the two pictures from the walls and laid them face down on the shelf of her closet.

There. Good.

She returned to the bed.

Now what?

Should she turn on the camera and say something? But what? She couldn't let viewers see her fear. Couldn't let on that anything was wrong. Ben would be watching. The man she loved so much.

Maybe she should just wait and see what the five o'clock clue said about her. If it was something she'd written on her application form, she'd know everything was okay.

Gina thrust a hand in her hair. Why hadn't she prayed more about coming on this show? She hadn't asked for God's guidance, not really. Her prayers had been more like: *I want to do this, God, so bless me, okay?* What if she really *had* sought His will? Would He have impressed upon her not to come?

Lord, now that I'm here, please help!

Gina sighed. She should be upstairs right now, talking to the other contestants. Trying to extract information from them. But she couldn't face anyone right now. Not until she was sure what was going on.

Which left only her own camera.

For the next fifteen minutes Gina paced her room, practicing what she would say. Something to make people like her. To see what a good person she was.

An idea hit. Gina played it over in her mind.

She opened the closet and brought out her wedding photo. Hung it above her bed, where the baby picture used to be.

Gina moved her suitcases to the floor so she could sit on the bed strategically, with the wedding photo over her right shoulder.

Here goes.

She took a deep breath and turned on the camera. A green light came on.

"Hi." She tried to smile. For a moment she hovered before the camera, then backed up to sit on the bed.

"I'm Gina." She swallowed. "Corrales. The real estate agent from L.A."

She turned her head left, then right. "I've just come into my room. So pretty in red and gold. They're the colors in the logo for my real estate agency. And the photo behind me — see it?" She indicated over her shoulder. "It's my wedding picture. So surprising to see it. But I understand why the show hung it here. My husband, Ben, is the most important person in the world to me. We've been married for fifteen years."

Suddenly all thought leaked from Gina's head. She opened and closed her mouth twice. Laughed nervously.

"I'm not used to talking to people I can't see. I'm usually with clients, finding out about their family and habits, what they need in a house. It's all about who *they* are. So it's kind of awkward to just ... talk alone about myself."

Gina fell silent again. The ticking seconds seemed interminable.

"I like to golf for a hobby. Actually, Ben and I do that together. But we're also kind of homebodies. We watch a lot of movies at home. Definitely film buffs. I always make a big bowl of popcorn —"

Gina felt her cheeks flush. She shouldn't have said that. People could already see she was way overweight. The last thing she needed was for them to envision her pigging out on anything.

What if they thought she was the sin of Gluttony just because she was too heavy? That would be so unfair.

Gina had grown up going to church. She knew all about the Seven Deadly Sins. And she was *not* one of them. So she liked to eat — so did lots of people. And she'd tried to lose weight countless times.

Oh, wonderful, she was staring at the camera like a deer in headlights. Gina blinked.

Surely they'd all guessed what she was thinking.

"I ... sorry. I'm just ... jet lagged." She forced another smile and knew it came out crooked. "I'll talk to you again a little later."

She jumped up and punched off the camera.

Leaning against the desk, Gina hung her head and fought back tears.

Chapter 8

Craig entered the kitchen to find Lance, Shari, and Tori making their lunches. Smells of deli meat and mayonnaise hung in the air. At the far end of the kitchen was a long eating counter with six stools. Their notebooks had been placed on the first, third and fourth of these stools.

Interesting.

Craig held his own notebook. Like the other contestants, he'd used the Sharpie to write his name on the cover. After every conversation, direct or overheard, all of them would be jotting down whatever information had been gleaned.

Imagine the anxiety of someone if their notebook went missing. The thought made Craig smile. He just might have to try stealing one.

All three people gave him a wary glance when he walked into the room. Man. What a different vibe from when they first got here. Then they were merely competitors. Now grim judgment swirled. Each looked at the other contestants as sinners, while trying to cover their own faults. Craig had never gone to church and knew little about the Bible. But didn't hidden sin inevitably give itself away, no matter how hard a person tried to hide it?

He plunked his notebook on the counter at stool number two. "Everybody just doing their own thing for food?"

"Apparently so." Lance held packages of cheese and meat. Beside him on the counter sat bread and various condiments.

Shari held up a small container and spoon. "I found yogurt."

Ugh. Her voice alone grated Craig's nerves.

Craig chose cheddar cheese and sliced beef and started making himself a sandwich. He looked around. "Where are the plates?"

Tori pointed to a cabinet close to the sink. Craig pulled out a plate.

Shari moved her notebook off the first stool and sat down, crossing her long tanned legs just so for viewers. The rest of them made their sandwiches in silence. Tension pulsed. Clearly they were all aware of the cameras, all acting. So much for being a "reality show."

Time for a little truth-seeking.

"Everybody find their rooms?" Craig sat down beside Shari with his filled plate and a napkin.

"I did." Lance took the stool next to him, with two sandwiches and a bowl full of chips.

"Me too," said Tori. She took the fourth seat, next to Lance.

"And me." Shari dipped the spoon into her yogurt.

Craig swallowed the first bite of sandwich. Good cheese, with a tang to it. "My room's nice. Obviously decorated for me. How did they know that?"

"I don't know." Tori's voice sounded a little too pinched. "But my room's the same way."

"Mine too." Lance wiped his mouth. "Which I find rather disconcerting. Obviously they know more than we told them."

The man was admitting this in front of the cameras.

"I have a question," Tori said. "The winner of the most votes at two o'clock receives a private clue on his or her own monitor. So ... are viewers told that clue?"

Craig frowned. "Aren't we supposed to talk into our own camera to say what question we want answered about another contestant? Viewers will hear that."

"But they won't know the answer unless we tell them. Right? Because the camera lens can't see what's on the monitor."

Lance shrugged. "Seems so."

Craig wiped his mouth. "Maybe the clue is listed on the show's website with all the others."

"You're probably right." Tori focused on the counter.

Craig studied her. Odd question.

"I don't know why you wouldn't want to tell viewers, anyway, just in case." Shari pushed aside her empty yogurt container. 'They'd be ticked if you didn't." She got up to throw her trash away.

Craig turned to Lance. "You have pictures on your walls?"

At the sink, Shari stiffened. Tori's hand stopped halfway to her plate, then resumed its movement.

"Do you?" Lance looked at him.

"Yeah. Three."

Lance nodded. "What are they?"

"You first."

"I asked you."

Craig eyed him, then lifted a shoulder. "The cover of *Gone With the Wind*, a child in leg braces, and a theater poster for the movie *Upside Out*."

Shari dropped her spoon.

All eyes turned toward her. Watching, assessing.

She shook her head. "Goodness. So clumsy." She picked the spoon up and tossed it into the sink.

Craig put down his sandwich. "That movie mean something to you?"

"No. Why should it? It's in *your* room."

"I saw that film." Tori narrowed her eyes at Shari. "Came out a couple years ago. You try out for a part in it?"

Shari shot her a look to kill. "Like I said, I don't know much about it."

"Is that a *no*?"

Craig watched Shari fight within herself over the answer. Because she was about to lie and feared getting caught?

"Yes." She wagged her head. "It means *no*. Now can I please be left in peace?"

Tori stuck her tongue under her top lip, still staring at Shari. Clearly not believing her. "That just might come back to bite you, honey." She picked up her notebook and left the kitchen. Probably to write it all down before she forgot.

Lance finished his last bite of sandwich and headed for the back deck, notebook stuck under his arm.

"Hey." Craig called after him. "So what are your three pictures?"

"Never said I'd answer."

"Oh, come on."

Lance waved a dismissive hand and lumbered out the door.

Jerk.

Lance's Notebook

June 4, 2013—Gina was realtor for couple buying house in Cheviot Hills, L.A. Who? Why matter?

March 2011—Craig's niece diagnosed with MS. Now 14. Sweet. Cheerful. Craig carries her picture. Started foundation after diagnosis. Where did he get the money? Wants to cure MS. Room pictures: Gone With the Wind, child in leg braces, Upside Out poster. Why pictures of GWTW and UO?

January 2014—Aaron to computer convention in L.A. So...?

April 2012—Shari auditions for Last Bend. Won part? Auditioned for Upside Out? (I think she lied.) Shari—Pride?

March 2012—I interview Bruce. **Why this clue??**

December 2001—Tori doesn't go to waitress job in Nashville. Tori—Sloth?

Chapter 9

Well, wasn't lunch fun. Shari was fuming. These people were sharks. Especially that Tori woman.

And that movie poster of *Upside Out* in Craig's room. *Why?*

Shari needed to keep calm, not let on that any of this was getting to her. Best way to do that? Keep talking to viewers. So, carrying her notebook, she took them on a tour of the rest of the house, chattering all the while. Ignoring the disdainful glances of the other contestants. They were just jealous of her ability with the cameras.

On the upper floor, besides the kitchen and great room, she found a den—without a television—and a small library. The laundry room was off the kitchen. Done with that level, Shari went downstairs and wandered out to the small backyard, which was surrounded by the gated fence they weren't supposed to cross.

"And that's the end of the tour." Shari stood on the back patio, facing a camera mounted on the corner post that supported the upper deck. "When you come right down to it, we can't really go anywhere but the house. I'd take you down to the beach, but I can't talk to you there. Mighty sad, if you ask me."

She lingered for a moment. What now?

Her thoughts flitted back to *Upside Out*. Did viewers think she'd lied about that movie, thanks to testy Tori?

Maybe she should fix it.

Shari headed back inside. As she reentered the house she heard voices in the hall that led to the bedrooms. She slowed in the entryway near the stairs and peeked around the corner. Gina stood near the door to the fifth room, keys in her hand. Talking to Aaron.

Shari pulled her head back and pressed against the wall, listening.

"… your clue." Aaron sounded almost accusing.

"What about it?"

"You had clients in June 2013 who bought a house in the Cheviot Hills neighborhood of L.A."

Silence.

"Who were they?"

Gina laughed. It sounded tinny. Some actress she'd make. "That was almost three years ago. How am I supposed to remember?"

"I think you remember just fine."

"Don't take that tone with me. I said I don't."

"And the photo hanging on the wall above your desk is a real estate *sold* sign."

Shari heard Gina suck in a breath. "What makes you say that?"

"Because it *is*."

"How do you *know* that? Have you been in my room?"

"How I know isn't important. I want to know why."

"*How* did you get in my *room*?"

"*Why* is it there?"

"I'm a *real estate agent*, what do you expect?"

"Fine. So who were your clients for Cheviot Hills?"

"What do you care?"

"Who were they?"

"Get out of my face!"

Shari heard the metallic sound of a key hitting a lock.

"*Who*, Gina?"

"Get away from me!"

A door slammed.

Shari wrenched from the wall and scurried on cat feet past the stairs. When she reached the back door she opened, then closed it with a bang. She turned around and headed toward the hallway as if just entering the house. Rounding the corner, she nearly ran into Aaron.

"Oh!" Shari jumped back.

Aaron's face was hard as metal. He barged past her without a word. Shari stood in the hall and listened to his feet pound up the stairs.

Her nerves rippled. First the movie poster in Craig's room of *Upside Out*. Now was there some connection between Aaron and Gina?

Shari slipped into her room and unlocked the sliding door. She slid it back, letting in the breeze. The curtains she opened only a little, in case people out on the deck tried to snoop. So much for the view. And it would be a pain having to close everything up every time she left. But she wouldn't take the chance of anyone getting into her room. Like Aaron.

Shari perched in the chair at her desk and flung open her notebook. She had to write things down, get her thoughts in order ...

When she was finished she wrote one question in big letters: *WHY?*

She leaned back in the chair, staring at the word.

Maybe it was all coincidence. Craig just liked the film *Upside Out*. Aaron had friends in Cheviot Hills and thought maybe Gina was their realtor.

But then why was Aaron so mad? And—out of the whole U.S. he had friends from one small neighborhood in L.A.? Aaron didn't even live in California. How likely was that, when George Fry had said fifty thousand people applied to be on *Dream Prize*?

Shari tossed down her pen. There had to be a normal explanation for this. Because otherwise it was way too freaky.

She tossed her head and tried to refocus. She'd wanted to come in here before two o'clock to talk to the viewers. Explain in a roundabout way why she'd dropped her spoon in the kitchen. She needed to get to it. And she couldn't show any fright.

I can do this.

Shari went into the bathroom to check her make-up. By the time she returned to the chair it was twenty minutes before two. No more time to mess around.

This topic wouldn't be easy.

After a deep breath, she turned on the camera and managed a bright smile.

"Hi, everyone! Shari Steele coming back to ya, now from my room." She rounded her eyes. "You saw that little spat between Aaron and Gina? What was *that* all about? And how did he know what was in her bedroom?" Shari effected a shiver. "Gonna be careful to lock my door, I can tell you that.

"Anyway, it's almost time for us to gather in the great room again. I just thought I'd let you know a little something about me in the meantime." She lowered her chin, looking at the camera from beneath her lashes. "The producer told you I'm an actress. Truth is, I had to leave California for over two years, just when my career was about to take off. In May of 2012 I learned my mother had been diagnosed with cancer. I'm her only child, and my dad walked away from our family a long time ago. So

I returned to Ohio to stay with her. At first we thought she might make it. She fought hard." Shari's eyes moistened, and her voice wavered. She straightened to gaze directly into the camera. "Mom fought for a long time. But then she got worse. By summer of 2014 I ... knew. She died in November." Shari looked away. "Soon after that I returned to L.A. And I've been trying to get my career going ever since." She smiled sadly. "It's not easy. There's a lot of people like me wanting the same thing. And leaving when I did was ... it just made things harder. But I'd do it all over again. Those years with my mom ... I wouldn't trade them for anything."

Shari blinked the tears away.

"Okay, I have to go now. See you upstairs."

She turned off the camera and sank back against the chair. Yay! She'd managed to get through her story.

A minute later Shari was fixing her makeup again at the bathroom mirror. Satisfied, she headed to the great room, notebook in hand. The other five contestants were already there. Gina still looked a little spooked. Aaron was calm but stone faced. What was with that guy, anyway? Lance was examining his notes. He looked up at her.

"That TV show you auditioned for—*Last Bend*. Is it still running?"

Shari hesitated. "No. It went three seasons. Ended last year."

"Which part did you try out for?"

Should she answer? Wouldn't viewers wonder if she didn't?

"Brittany Ayres. The lead."

Gina nodded. "I watched the first season of that."

"I saw all three seasons," Tori said.

Well, good for her.

"Who got the part?" Lance just wouldn't quit pushing. But this was going too far. Besides, it was complicated. Shari turned away.

"That actress who was in …" Gina snapped her fingers.

"Evy Barring." Tori sounded like such a know-it all, just because she ran some big company. "That was her name."

Lance opened his notebook and wrote in it. Gina, Tori, Craig, and Aaron did the same.

"So what?" Shari tossed her head. "None of that's important."

They ignored her.

The hands of the sun ray clock on the wall moved to two.

Please let me win the most votes!

They all huddled around the dark screen, waiting for it to come to life. Shari breathed another prayer that she'd see her own name. The question she wanted to ask as an extra clue was burning a hole in her brain.

Suddenly the monitor came to life. Faint light moved across it, growing brighter and morphing into the Dream Prize logo. The graphic hung there for interminable seconds, then faded. Words appeared on the screen.

This round's majority of votes go to Shari Steele.

What?

"Yes!" Shari raised a fist and grinned at a camera. "Thank you! Thank you *so* much!"

The screen went black.

"How nice for you," Craig said. Sarcasm dripped off the words. He arched his back and looked around, like he couldn't even figure out what to do next. Then he left the room.

Gina and Tori were eyeing Shari like she'd stuffed the ballot box or something. Lance shrugged—*what do you expect?* He wandered out of the room toward the kitchen. Aaron wrote in his notebook. Probably her name—and how she didn't deserve the win.

Well, wasn't everyone just full of congratulations.

Fact was, the whole room had a really bad vibe. Like these people weren't just her competitors, they were her sworn enemies.

Shari lifted a shoulder. Fine then. She saw that kind of backbiting in Hollywood every day.

With a wag of her head, she went down to her bedroom to hear her extra clue.

Not bothering to open her sliding door or curtains, Shari turned on her camera and again thanked everyone who'd voted for her. "And now for my extra clue, I'd like to know something about Craig. What significance does the movie *Upside Out* have for him?"

She gazed expectantly at her monitor.

It stayed dark.

Ten seconds ticked by.

Twenty.

Shari waited a forever minute. Talk about boring the viewers.

"This is taking way too long." She sighed. "Somebody thousands of miles from here has to find the answer and type it in, I guess. I'm gonna turn off the video until it appears. Then I'll let you know what it says."

She hit the button on the camera, and the green light went out.

"Come on, come on." Shari opened her notebook, pen in hand.

Finally the *Dream Prize* logo appeared on her monitor. Then disappeared, followed by text.

Your question has been registered. To find the answer, go through the backyard gate and follow the path about fifty yards. Don't let anyone see you leave. You will not be penalized for going outside the fence. You'll come to a small shed with a door. Go inside, down the steps, and through the next door. You'll find a room with a table in the center. On that table is a monitor with your extra clue. Take your notebook.

Shari blinked at the words. What? She didn't want to do all that. She just wanted her extra clue. What a total pain. Why couldn't they just give the answer here?

Nothing about this show was turning out to be easy.

Grumbling to herself, she picked up her notebook and left the room, locking the door behind her. The key slid into her shorts pocket. At the back door she slipped outside. If anyone was out on the upper kitchen deck, they might see her going through the gate. What then?

She eased beyond the patio into the backyard, turned around and looked upward. No one there. By the time she reached the gate, would she be visible through a kitchen window? Shari hesitated, weighing her decision. Then abruptly turned and headed for the gate. She went through as fast as possible and followed the path into the dense bushes and trees.

Away from the house, she felt some of the tension leave her shoulders. If only she could stay out here.

Before long she reached the shed. Didn't look like much, but it had a thick door. Maybe an underground storm shelter or something. They were high enough above water level up on this hill to make that possible. Shari pulled back the heavy door and spotted concrete stairs leading down into the earth, dimly lit by a single bulb. A trap door that would cover the stairs had been pulled back and lay against the ground in the shed. Shari squinted down the stairs. At the bottom was another heavy-looking door. Spooky.

A shudder ran through her.

What if she just didn't do this?

She hesitated a moment longer, then stepped over the threshold but didn't want to pull the door completely shut behind her. She eased it closed without latching it.

The air smelled icky musty. It took a minute for her vision to adjust from the bright sunlight.

The door behind her banged shut.

Shari whirled around.

How—?

She slapped a hand on the door to push it open, then stopped.

Okay, this was really creepy. But she was too much of a fighter to let it get to her. She'd do what she needed and get out of here as fast as possible.

Shari hurried down the stairs. At the bottom she opened the second door, this time being more careful that it wouldn't latch behind her.

She entered a cool, barren-looking room, maybe twenty feet square. Concrete block floor and walls. Some chairs and a refrigerator. What was this place, a bunker? Gave her the total willies. Maybe next time she wouldn't even *want* to win the most votes. Not if it meant coming here again.

In the middle of the room sat a table with a monitor, just like she'd been told. Shari walked to it.

Behind her, the door clicked shut.

Shari jumped. *No!*

She dropped her notebook and ran to the door. Pushed against it. Didn't move.

She pushed again, twisting the handle, leaning against the wood with all her might. It *wouldn't move.*

The door was *locked.*

Panic poured over Shari's head. She banged on the door with both fists. "Hey! Let me *out*!" She pounded and kicked and pushed and screamed. But it didn't budge. And who would hear her? She pounded more until her fists hurt and her energy ran out.

Gasping, Shari slid to the floor, her back against the door. She buried her head in her hands, forcing herself to *breathe*. Long and slow. Get control of herself. All she had to do was get the clue. Then the door would unlock, let her out of there. If she ever had to do this again, she would prop both doors wide open.

"Okay." Shari sputtered through her fingers. "Okay. Just … get up."

She pushed herself to stand, legs trembling. Brushing sweat from her face, she forced herself to walk to the table. The monitor was black.

Shari pushed the *on* button.

The screen lightened. But no words appeared.

"Come on. *Please.*" Her voice shook.

Shari stood before the stubborn screen.

Waiting.

Watching.

Long minutes dragged by.

She trotted to the door and tried again to open it. Didn't work. She banged on it, shouting, terror rising, coursing through her body. Somewhere along the way she totally lost it. She started flinging herself back and forth between the door and table. Rattling the lock, slapping the monitor. Back and forth, then back again. Kicking the door. Screaming. Yelling at the grey screen to *say something*!

Her voice went hoarse.

Nothing came on the monitor. Nothing. And she couldn't. Get. *Out*!

Shari collapsed into a chair and sobbed.

Chapter 10

Lance was in the kitchen, enjoying a bag of potato chips, when he spotted a flash of red through the window. He walked to the sliding glass door and looked out to see Shari in the backyard near the gate. She was walking quickly and carried her notebook. Reaching the gate, she slipped through and disappeared.

Ah, another puzzlement. What was she doing? She'd just lost half the day's votes. And after being so happy about winning the most not ten minutes ago.

"See something interesting?"

A voice behind Lance made him jump. He turned to see Tori placing her notebook on the center island.

"Just the backyard. Pretty out there." He held out the potato chip bag. "Care to indulge?"

"No thanks." She sighed. "I might take a diet soda." She pulled a can from the fridge.

Lance studied Tori. He still smarted from losing the most votes to Plastic Shari. And the morning clue about his "secret" continued to haunt him. He must gather his wits, uncover others' information. And he had only two and half days to draw his conclusions.

He sat down two seats away from Tori, placing the bag of chips before him. "So in 2001 you had the esteemed employment of waiting tables."

Tori stilled, the glass halfway to her lips. "Is that supposed to be a sarcastic remark?"

"Not at all."

She eyed him. "Then yes. I was a waitress."

"I'd say you've come a long way since then."

"True."

"Why didn't you report to work that day? In December, wasn't it?"

Tori gazed at him, as if surprised he remembered the details. "I was sick."

Lance nodded slowly. "Strange clue to give about you, fifteen years ago. Sounds so insignificant."

No response.

The key to pulling a story out of someone was empathy—and the dangled carrot of more to come. Make the person believe her story would touch many who heard it. They would identify with her, *feel* her. Want her to succeed.

"Clearly it wasn't," he said. "Insignificant, that is."

Tori took a long drink of soda. "Like I said, I was sick."

"With what?"

She shrugged.

"Something serious?"

"You could say that."

"Did you ever return to your waitressing job?"

Tori focused out the window. "No."

Ah.

"When did you recover?"

Tori turned to him in exasperation. "I don't have to answer your questions, you know."

"True." Lance pointed to a camera. "But they want to hear. They're playing this game along with us, remember? They want to win, too. And if you say nothing about yourself all week, they're not likely to warm to you."

"Well, then, why don't we talk about *you*?"

Lance crunched on potato chips, then wiped his fingers on a napkin. "I propose an agreement . You answer my questions, I'll answer yours."

Tori narrowed her eyes.

"I will. Promise."

She looked away and sipped on her drink.

"So, tell me. When did you recover?"

She sighed again. Seconds ticked by. Lance was beginning to think she'd refused to participate.

Tori set down her glass with a *clink*. "April of the following year."

"That was a long illness." Lance raised his eyebrows. "Where did you work after that?"

"I went to school." Tori's voice firmed. "I'd never had the chance to go. So I enrolled in college and majored in business. Got my B.A., then went on to grad school, waitressing at different restaurants all the while. Took me eight years. But in 2010 I had my Masters."

"An impressive story. Good for you. You've made quite a success of yourself. So when did you start working for your current software company?"

"Right after I graduated."

Since 2010. She'd been there six years and had worked her way up to vice president. Lance slid another chip into his mouth. So what was so important about missing that day of work fifteen years ago?

Had to be the illness. Something she did not want known.

"You married, Tori?"

She gave a sad smile. "No."

"Ever been?"

"This is a *lot* of questions! I'd say it's time I quizzed you."

"Just one more. Were you ever married?"

Tori's expression flattened. "Yes, okay? Before I ... got sick. He was in med school. *I* worked to support us."

Bitterness tinged her words. And at that moment Lance saw through successful businesswoman Tori Hattinger. Saw the pain in her heart. He softened his voice. "He left you, didn't he. Once he had the title *Doctor.* Maybe even took up with someone else."

Tori shot Lance a withering look, then seemed to recover. Her shoulders pulled back. "Real original, huh. Must be the plot point for dozens of movies."

Lance let that hang in the air, imagining his audience. Not just listening, but *watching.* "Movies represent life. The human condition. And unfortunately, that kind of betrayal happens all too often."

No comment.

So what was her illness? Nervous breakdown? Depression? Lance toyed with a potato chip. So what? Who couldn't understand someone in those circumstances experiencing tremendous grief and pain?

He put the chip in his mouth, barely tasting it.

Perhaps whatever "secrets" they all were afraid would be revealed weren't so menacing after all. Which meant whatever his "secret" was, it couldn't involve Bruce Egan. The morning clue was, indeed, coincidence.

Tori drained the last of her soda. "Okay, your turn."

Lance spread his hands—*at your service.*

She got up and read inside her notebook. Returned to her seat. "Who was the man you interviewed who'd successfully gone through drug rehab?"

Great. Lance raised a shoulder. "That was four years ago. And I only used his first name on the radio at the time, so that's all I should mention here. But they must be talking about Bruce."

"Did he come to your station, so you met him in person?"

"Yes."

"Why is that interview so important?"

"I don't know. I'm on the radio five days a week, and I interview a lot of people. He was someone who had gone through a fairly new local rehab facility in the Sacramento area. I remember being impressed with its program. Nothing more than that."

Tori drew back her head and regarded Lance. "You know you'll lose points if you're caught lying."

"Lying? Moi?"

"I think you are. When you heard that clue this morning, you reacted. There's something about this man that's important to you."

Lance felt his face go hot. "It was important news for our community. That's the extent of it."

"Did *you* ever need drug rehab?"

"No."

"Rehab for alcohol?"

"No rehab. For anything."

"Ever see Bruce again?"

Lance hesitated. "No."

Tori gave him a knowing look, then turned to face a camera. "I think he did, don't you? Mr. Fry, why don't you speak to that in your next clue about him?"

"Hey!" Lance slapped the counter. "That's not part of our agreement."

"What — trying to drive the game? It's what I do. I lead employees in a large company. Show them the direction to go next."

"But this — "

"Didn't you just do what *you* do, Mr. Radio Interviewer? Try to draw information out of me? Tell me this." Tori leaned closer. "Which of the Seven Deadly Sins do *you* represent?"

"None. One of us has a pass, remember?"

"*Maybe* one of us does. And if it's anyone — it's me."

Tori stood up and walked closer to the camera in the far corner of the kitchen. "Do me a favor out there? Give me your votes this time around. And when I win, I'll ask for an extra clue about Lance. To be exact — *when* did he see Bruce again? And under what circumstances?"

Tori turned back and aimed Lance a satisfied smile.

Shrew.

He was sweating hard. Viewers could surely see the perspiration on his face. Never had anyone so turned the tables on him during an interview. But ultimately this wasn't even about him. This was about his *son.*

Lance pushed to his feet, snatching up the half eaten bag of chips. "Or you all could vote for *me.*" He nodded at the camera, mouth tight. "And I'll ask what 'illness' the estimable Tori Hattinger suffered — and exactly what about that illness she needs to hide."

Tori folded her arms and glared at him. Lance fumed right back. This woman had gone too far, and he would take her down for it. No one threatened his family. *No one.*

Chapter 11

Aaron stomped around the beach. Nothing was going right. Miss Hollywood Priss getting the most votes? Couldn't viewers see right through her? Stupid people. And Gina was lying about not remembering the house in Cheviot Hills.

If that house was the one he thought ...

Aaron bent over and spat in the water.

At one time he'd vowed to kill the realtor involved with that house if he ever saw her. Could she possibly be on this island? In this show?

What were the odds?

He *would* find out what was going on.

Aaron trudged back to the house and into his closed-up bedroom. He needed to study his notes before the next set of clues. So far he had to know more than anyone else. He was the only one who'd seen their bedrooms—except for Craig's. And the pictures in every room were important. He knew that even more now. Look how Gina had reacted to his questions.

He sat at his desk and read his notes, focusing on the photos above each person's desk. *Tori—ambulance. Shari—herself with friend.* Who was that? Somebody Aaron had seen before. Another actress? *Lance —courtroom. Gina — sold sign.*

Aaron thought of his own desk photo, shoved under his bed. The restaurant. Where they'd had dinner. And he'd heard the news. He'd stormed out ...

Aaron took a long, deep, breath. In, out.

In.

Out.

Okay. He was good.

He looked back to his notes. Shari? He still thought she was Pride. And now he had an idea about Gina.

He needed certain questions answered. Only way to make sure that happened? Win the most votes. Aaron eyed the camera. Chattering to viewers like Shari? Disgusting thought.

But he *had* to win votes.

Did viewers like arguments?

Aaron cocked his head. Maybe they did. All those sleazy reality shows—weren't they all about people fighting?

Getting along was boring.

Well, then.

He got up for a drink of water, then turned on his camera. Lowered himself into the desk chair. "Hi, Aaron here, with exclusive information for you. You saw me sneaking into bedrooms? I will tell you what I found ...

Aaron went over every picture in each room. What kind of meaning they might have, based on their placement on the walls. He did not mention his picture of the restaurant.

"Now—Gina. She lied about not remembering that house she sold. You saw how she acted. Don't waste votes on her. If a clue proves she *does* know what house I'm talking about, she'll lose half her votes anyway. Vote for me. I'll keep things interesting. Report everything I know." He nodded curtly. "Thanks."

Aaron turned off the camera. He opened his sliding door and walked outside. He gazed at the ocean, thinking of Lisa. Dreaming of their yacht.

A few minutes before five o'clock, Aaron climbed the stairs to the great room. His stomach fluttered. How bad would his second clue be?

Lance, Tori, Craig, and Gina were already standing near the table. Gina sent him a scathing glance, then looked away. Lance and Tori didn't seem to be getting along too well, either.

One happy family. And this was only the first day.

The clock read five.

They formed a semicircle around the monitor. The air crackled. That first batch of clues had hit them all hard. And now?

"Where's Shari?" Tori looked toward the door.

Craig shook his head. "Don't know."

"Me either," Gina said.

Lance frowned.

Aaron stayed silent. Miss Hollywood thought she was so great with the cameras, she didn't need clues?

Light played across the monitor.

Here we go. Aaron gripped his pen until he thought it might break.

DREAM PRIZE

Sunday 5 p.m.

During the last weekend of July 2013, *Gina's* husband, Ben, was out of town on a camping trip with two friends from college.

~~~

In June 2013, *Craig* hired an accountant for his foundation.

~~~

In May 2013, *Aaron's* father, Shan Wang, accepted a job in Los Angeles, California.

~~~

In May 2012, *Shari* learned her roommate at the time, Kathryn Flex, landed the part Shari had tried out for in the TV show *Last Bend*.

~~~

On October 23, 2012, the man from the rehab facility, whom *Lance* had interviewed in March, testified in a trial in which the defendant was accused of stealing $50,000.

~~~

From July to October 2013, *Tori* dated a man ten years her junior.

Chapter 12

Nate.

The name echoed in Tori's head, along with the stuttered breathing of the other contestants.

Nate West.

Her clue about dating a younger man hung on the screen, mocking her. And the rest clearly mocked the other contestants, for reasons Tori couldn't yet know.

Nobody moved.

Aaron broke the stillness, pressing his pen hard against paper as he wrote. Lance was staring at his notebook blankly, stunned. Craig mumbled something under his breath and began to write. Gina dropped her pen. Picked it up and dropped it again.

Write, Tori.

She set her jaw and began to take notes. She'd skimmed the other clues in looking for her own. Now as she scribbled down the second on the list, her hand stilled. *Craig hired an accountant in June 2013.*

An accountant. For his multiple sclerosis foundation. Which must be in Malibu, close to where Craig lived.

Understanding barreled through Tori.

What?

Why hadn't that foundation clicked in her mind before—given all the times she'd traveled to Southern California on business? The accountant had to be *him*.

Her body swayed.

Tori swallowed and forced herself to keep writing. But the fourth clue brought her hand to another halt. Kathryn Flex—that actress who'd recently become so popular after starring in *Upside Out*—used to be *Shari's roommate*? Is that why Shari dropped her spoon when she heard Craig had a poster of the movie in his room?

Was this another connection? Craig and Shari?

But that was a stretch. Craig probably just liked the movie. So had Tori. And Kathryn Flex was now famous after her debut movie was such a hit, so everyone knew who she was.

The tie between Tori and Craig was different ...

She wrenched her mind back to her task. The fifth clue stopped Tori once more. That man Lance had interviewed—Bruce—later testified at a trial about the theft of $50,000.

Lance had obviously lied when Tori asked him if he'd ever seen Bruce again. She pictured Lance sitting on the kitchen stool, breaking out in sweat. So was this trial where Lance saw him? But why would Lance be in the courtroom?

Had *he* been the defendant accused of stealing?

Tori's mind spun. So much to consider. But not now. She could only push on with taking notes. The last clue was her own. She wrote it down word for word.

Just as she finished, the monitor faded to black.

She stepped away from the table, her ankles weak.

That emotion—weakness—was *unacceptable*. Tori Hattinger had long ago vowed nobody—especially any man—would make her feel that way again. Whatever this show thought it was doing, she wasn't going to take it.

She'd dealt with adversity before. Had looked deep into the well of unfairness—and risen above it all. Now *she* was the one in control.

Tori smacked her notebook shut and looked up, catching a look at Gina. The woman was downright pale.

"What *is* this?" Tori whirled and faced a camera. "What do you want from us, George Fry?" She pointed at the lens. "All of you watching—this show isn't what they say it is. It's … taunting. He's saying things that aren't—" Tori snapped her mouth closed. Come off too strong, and they'd think she was losing it. That she had something to hide. She turned away.

Lance headed for the nearest sofa and sank into it. He clasped his hands between his legs. Stared at the floor. His clue had clearly gotten to him. Served him right for the way he'd treated her.

Good chance to move viewers' attention off herself.

Tori strode toward him. "So, Bruce-the-ex-druggie again, right, Lance? Were you at that trial?"

Lance didn't move. Sweat trickled down his temple.

"Did Bruce testify against somebody? Maybe *you?*"

Lance raised his chin. Rage shone in his eyes. "You have no idea what you're talking about."

"Do tell."

"Shut *up*, Tori."

"Well, aren't you—"

Aaron's voice cut through the room. "*Who* were your clients who bought that house?"

Tori jerked her head around to see him glaring at Gina. The realtor had one hand pressed to the side of her neck.

"*Tell* me!"

Craig took a step toward them. "What're you talking about?"

"None of your business. *She* knows. Look at her face."

Gina moved her hand to her chest. Tears glistened in her eyes.

Tori glanced from her to Aaron. What was happening? Tori's own clue was definitely connected to Craig's. Now what was this between Aaron and Gina?

Aaron gestured with his notebook. "I will find out what you're hiding, Gina. I bet you know what I'm thinking. And if I'm right ... you'd better watch your back."

Gina's expression flattened, like a bullied kid who'd been pushed too far. "Is that a *threat*?"

"Take it however you want."

"You're *threatening* me on national TV?" She took a step toward Aaron. He moved to her until they stood inches apart, breathing hard. He was a good half foot taller.

"Whoa, wait a minute." Craig moved in. "Both of you, back off."

Lance pushed from the couch, watching them as if he might have to wade in and stop a fight.

Gina stepped away. Licked her lips. "I want off this game." She pivoted toward a camera. "You hear me? I want out!"

"You can't get out." Lance's voice thickened. "The boat's long gone."

"It can come back. They can send it."

"It *won't* come back until Tuesday." Lance spread his hands, his face creasing. "We're stuck here—in whatever kind of craziness this show is throwing at us."

Aaron eyed Lance. "Are your clues connected to someone else here?"

"No. Are yours?"

Aaron's gaze shifted to Craig. "How about you?"

"No." He lifted a shoulder.

Relief flooded Tori. Craig didn't know. But there was no reason he should.

She took a breath. "I'm not connected to anyone either."

Aaron turned his brooding focus on her. His fingers twitched. "I don't believe you. I don't believe *any* of you. Because something's going on here." He trained in again on Gina. She managed to stand her ground. "You want to tell them who your clients were who bought that house in Cheviot Hills? Huh?"

"I *told* you. I don't remember."

"What's my last name? Wang. I know it's common. But now you've heard *my father's* name."

Gina's cheeks turned pink. "I don't talk about my clients publicly. Just because someone used me as their realtor doesn't mean they have to have their name announced on national TV."

"You just said you didn't *remember* who they were."

Gina's mouth opened, then closed.

"That's half her day's votes." Aaron jabbed his finger toward a camera. "She *lied*."

Tori glanced at Craig. His brows were knit. Lance edged closer, as if this argument would shed light on his own concerns.

"I'm done here." Gina tried to move around Aaron.

He stepped in her path.

"Get out of my way."

"*Who* were your clients?"

"Get. Out. Of my way!"

Gina tried to push past him. Aaron grabbed her arm. "You sold that house to my *parents*!"

Gina wrenched away. "That's impossible."

"Shan Wang. Tell me you don't remember him."

Fake surprise pinned itself on Gina's face. She straightened her clothing. "Oh. Yes. Now that you mention it, maybe I do."

Aaron's neck reddened.

"And maybe I'm beginning to recall the house. Vaguely. Nice neighborhood. Good fit for my clients." Gina lasered Aaron with her eyes. "Now, as I said. I *don't* talk about my clients." She looked up toward a camera. "You all are witnesses. This man has threatened me. Grabbed me. I demand a boat be sent to take me off this island." She shook her notebook at the camera. "And if anything more happens to me, I will *sue* you."

Aaron made a disgusted sound in his throat. "I know which of the Seven Deadly Sins *you* are."

He pivoted on his heel and stomped outside to the deck. Tori heard his hard footfalls against the curving stairs.

Gina's sin? Which one would that be? As for Aaron, Tori was beginning to bet on Wrath.

Gina leaned against the center table and put her head in her hands.

Tori patted her arm. "You all right?"

She jerked up. "No, I'm not all right! I'm done playing this spiteful 'game.' That man's a maniac." She pointed toward the deck. "Plus we've been dumped here with no help. And by the way—*where* is Shari?"

That *was* a mystery.

Craig frowned. "That clue about Shari. Her roommate used to be Kathryn Flex? Wow."

A realization hit Tori. The clue said Kathryn Flex got the part Shari had wanted in *Last Bend*, which according to Shari was the lead. But Kathryn didn't star in *Last Bend*. Evy Barring did …

"Don't you think we should be concerned?" Gina aimed her words toward a camera. "Maybe Aaron threatened her, too, and now she's disappeared. Why wouldn't she show up for the clues?"

"I saw her." Lance said. "Right after the two o'clock announcement."

Gina turned to him. "Where?"

"She went out the rear gate."

"You mean outside the fence?"

Lance nodded. "Looked like she was on a mission. She didn't hesitate."

Tori considered the information. "Why would she do that? It would cost her half today's votes. And right after she was so excited about getting the most."

"I don't know. I was intrigued as well. But I thought, hey, it's *her* votes. Now that she's been gone so long, and with everything else ... I don't know."

Craig looked toward the ocean. "The sun will set in, what? An hour and a half? She ought to get back before then."

"But where could she even go?" Gina ran a hand across her forehead. "This island's not that big."

She was right. The island had looked quite small to Tori as their boat approached that morning. "What if she got hurt? Maybe she needs our help."

"But we'd have to go outside the fence to look for her," Lance said. "We'll lose votes."

"Yes, but if it's for someone's safety ..."

Gina scoffed. "Like the people who run this show care."

Craig walked closer to the window, gazing at the beach. "Maybe she had a very good reason for going. Maybe she's back and in her room right now."

"Anyone know what room she's in?" Tori looked from Craig to Lance. They both shook their heads.

Gina nodded. "Third one."

"Okay. I'll go check." Tori left the room, relieved to be out of there. Her mind still roiled as she descended the stairs. Gina and Aaron—clearly connected. Now she and Craig. The work this show had done to dig all this up. And this was only the first day.

Queasiness rolled through Tori's stomach.

At the third room she knocked on the door. "Shari?"

Silence.

She knocked again. "Shari?"

Nothing.

Tori tried the handle. Locked.

She leaned against the wall and closed her eyes. What now? Should she look for Shari? And as for Tori's own clue—what if Craig later realized his connection with her? What would he do? Would he care?

Tori dragged herself back to the great room to report she couldn't find Shari. Then she returned downstairs to her room, where she collapsed on her bed. She lay there a good half hour before finding the energy to get up and try to make sense of it all in her notebook. She *would* figure out what was happening here.

If the show didn't destroy her first.

Tori's Notebook

Gina:

June 2013: Gina is realtor for Aaron's parents. They buy house in Cheviot Hills, CA. Aaron furious about this.
July 2013: Gina's husband on camping trip with friends.
??—camping trip-so what?
??—why Aaron so mad?

Craig:

March 2011: Craig's niece diagnosed with MS
June 2013: Craig hires accountant for MS foundation—**Nate**
??—Why this clue? Why is show tying me/Craig, Gina/Aaron?

Aaron:

May 2013: Aaron's father accepts job in L.A.
June 2013: Gina sells parents house in L.A. neighborhood
January 2014: Aaron attends computer convention, L.A.

??—why convention clue? Visit parents while there? (Aaron lives in Texas.)

Shari:
April 2012-auditioned for Last Bend
May 2012-roommate Kathryn Flex gets part. But doesn't star in show. Evy Barring does. ??
Late 2013 (?) Movie Upside Out releases. Stars Kathryn. Big hit.
??—what happened between May 2012 and late 2013?

Lance:
March 2012: interviewed Bruce (drug rehab) on radio show
October 2012: Bruce testifies in trial about theft of $50K
??—is trial where Lance saw Bruce again? Why is Lance there?

Me:
2001: no-show at waitressing job
July to October 2013: date Nate
??—does show know I didn't go to work because of second suicide attempt?
??-why put these two clues together?

Chapter 13

In the dim bunker Shari slumped on one of the gray folding chairs, staring at the concrete floor. She'd cried herself out. Screamed herself out. And thrown up everything in her stomach. Now she felt like a limp rag. And she was cold. The place had to be ten degrees cooler than outside.

Her watch said five-fifteen. She'd been in this nightmare for three hours. And she'd come to realize something absolutely terrifying.

No one would come looking for her.

First of all, they had no idea where she was. Besides, who would risk losing votes to cross the fence? Like the other contestants cared? They cared only about themselves. Which is why they were here in the first place, according to George Fry. They represented horrible sins.

You have a sin of your own.

Not true. Shari scrubbed away the thought.

She leaned back against the chair, head tipped up. If only she'd stopped to tell viewers what the instructions that appeared on her monitor had said. Now even they couldn't know she was down here. They had to be wondering why she never came back on camera to tell them the answer she'd received to her question about Craig.

The only hope left for Shari now was the end of the game on Tuesday afternoon, when the boat captain returned. The show would be over, and one of the other five would be the winner. *Then* they would look for her. Surely the captain would do that. He'd been paid to bring them here—and take them back. He wouldn't just leave her behind.

Two more days. That was an eternity.

Shari moaned. She just might start gagging again.

She pushed to her feet and shuffled to the refrigerator. Opened it and counted the water bottles for the fourth time. Still twelve. Water ran in the bathroom sink. She could drink that if she had to. But was it safe? The bigger problem might be the food. There were some packets of lunch meat and cheese. A few pieces of fruit. That was it. Enough to last her until Tuesday. But if she *wasn't* found then ...

Something *pinged.*

Shari whirled around.

A light was glowing from the monitor.

She sucked in a breath and ran to the table. Gripped its edge and bent over to watch the screen, heart tripping.

The *Dream Prize* logo filled the screen, followed by a list of the five o'clock clues.

Shari leaned in closer. The clues? *Here?*

Why? How?

Did they *know* she was still in here?

She drew her head back. Trying to think.

Maybe *all* the clues would show up here, as long as the screen was turned on. But no one in their right mind would choose to stay in this place.

A stunning thought hit her. Was she *supposed* to be trapped in this bunker?

Shari dug fingers into her scalp. There had to be another explanation ...

But none would come.

Why else would the clues be showing up on this screen? Meanwhile the extra one she'd come here for had never appeared. Had those instructions on her bedroom monitor been just a trick to *get* her here?

Anger and disgust and hope spurted through Shari at once. If those doors had been jimmied to lock behind her automatically, this was more than just a TV show. This was some sick kind of torture.

But at least they'd let her out at some point. And for now, these clues kept her in the game —

Shari blinked. She had to write them down before they faded.

Her head jerked right and left, her gaze landing on the notebook she'd dropped three hours ago. She snatched it up. Her mind still spun, but she had to focus. Breathing hard, she began writing down the clues.

Number four—the one about her—stopped her cold. For a long moment she couldn't move.

Shari, keep at it!

She managed to scribble down the final clue just as the monitor went blank.

Shari threw her notebook on the table and pressed both hands to her cheeks. Her thoughts curled in on themselves, knotting into a giant ball.

That clue about her roommate, Kathryn Flex, getting the part in the TV show she had auditioned for. What that had led to ...

Shari scuttled sideways and fell into a chair. Clutching both arms to her chest, she leaned forward, rocking, rocking. This couldn't be what it looked like. It *couldn't*.

The first clue had been about her audition. Now this second about Kathryn. Plus the *Upside Out* movie poster in Craig's room. They all pointed toward one thing. Almost like George Fry *knew* ...

How *could* he know? Nobody did. If someone found out, she was done. Her dreams of being an actress, her *life* would be flat over.

Shari sucked air into her lungs. This had to be coincidence. So it was stuff about her career, so what? Anyone checking into her background could find it out.

But deep down Shari didn't believe that. Something was up here.

Was Kathryn behind this? Now she was Miss Movie Star after her lead in *Upside Out*. Miss I-Made-It-Big, while ex-roomie Shari struggled to pay the bills with walk-on parts. What if Kathryn had met George Fry? What if they'd schemed this?

But that would mean Kathryn *knew*. Which was impossible.

And Craig—why was the *Upside Out* poster in his room? What did he have to do with that movie? Shari was supposed to have been told that in her extra clue. She'd *earned* that answer.

Shari cursed aloud. How dare this show cheat her! How *dare* they trap her here, scare her until she puked? Was this their idea of entertainment? Just wait till she got home. She'd sue George Fry and his Sensation Network for everything they owned. This was beyond ridiculous. Nobody deserved to be treated like this.

Shari got up and paced the bunker, indignation tasting like metal in her mouth. She stomped around and around the table, until her burst of energy drained away. Finally she stumbled to the refrigerator and pulled out a bottle of water. Sat down hard in a chair and guzzled it all.

And then—a new thought streaked through her mind.

Shari's fingers let the empty water bottle slip. It hit the floor with a hollow *pop*, then bounced. Slowly she straightened, moving her wary gaze over the walls.

If her being trapped here was planned, if this was part of *Dream Prize's* sick idea of entertainment—where was the camera?

Chapter 14

"*So what* if my clients for that Cheviot Hills house were Aaron's parents?" Gina perched in the chair at her desk, waving her arms. The soft green *on* light of her private camera hardly made her feel serene. Inside she was a glowing ball of lava. She didn't even try to keep her voice from shaking. Why not let the viewers see how enraged she was? "I'm not even sure they were. He's right—Wang is a very common Chinese last name. But even if he *is* right, what's he so upset about? I do remember now that it was a nice home, and my clients were very happy to find it so quickly. I helped them negotiate a good deal." Gina smacked the desk with her fist. "Another satisfied customer."

She shook her head, then gazed out her open sliding door. The sun was lowering above the ocean. It would be dark in an hour.

Gina looked back to the camera. "I'm telling you that guy Aaron is crazy. Don't believe a word he says. Tell you something else—I'm staying as far away from him as I can. Plus I'm not going to take his lack of respect any more. I did nothing to deserve being treated like this."

She heaved a sigh. "Okay. I'm done for now. Besides, my stomach is talking to me. I've barely eaten anything today, and it's time for dinner. See you in the kitchen."

With a tight nod, she turned off the camera.

The second the green light faded, Gina fell back in her chair and let out a long breath. She still shook inside. Had she hidden her fear well enough behind the anger? They *had* to believe her. Especially Ben.

But God knew the truth. Gina's conscience screamed at her.

She raised her eyes toward the ceiling. "What do You expect me to do, Jesus? Admit my horrible mistake on national television? It's in the past. I'll never do it again. You've forgiven me. *Why* are You letting this come up now?"

Gina hung there a moment, then got up and moved to stand before the open sliding door. The warm breeze tickled her face. She closed her eyes and tried to enjoy its tropical sensation, but her soul could not be calmed.

Couldn't this thing with Aaron still be coincidence? He seemed to think everyone else in the show might be connected somehow, but they didn't appear to be.

But his *father*. Shan Wang. Gina squeezed her eyes shut.

What was Ben thinking about all this? He had to be furious at seeing her attacked like that, while he was so far away with no ability to protect her. That would hurt him.

Gina's throat tightened. Ben was a good man. He didn't deserve to be hurt. She'd never wanted to hurt him. And she would *not* hurt him now.

She turned to study the camera. What if she told viewers why her dream prize was the ten million in cash—and the first thing she planned to do with it? That would gain her votes, especially from women. Pull on their heartstrings. As it should. A woman who'd suffered three miscarriages, who was now thirty-nine and longed *so much* to give her loving husband a baby—viewers would want her to have that. She'd tell them about the new medical breakthrough that might cure her womb. The surgery that cost far more than she and Ben could ever pay ...

But she couldn't do it.

Gina swung back to the outside view. Her dream prize was too private, the subject of many intimate conversations between her and Ben. How would he feel to watch her tell millions of people their deepest desire— just to win their votes?

She sighed. Two more days of this. Her time for gathering information and solving the show was short, yet emotionally it seemed an eternity. Somehow she had to pull herself together. And *win.*

She headed for the bathroom, where she spent five minutes freshening her makeup. When she finished she only felt more miserable. Gina gazed at herself in the mirror, wishing for the millionth time her eyes weren't so small, her lashes so short. Her face was pretty but fat, and her body was way too big. What it must feel like to be narrow-waisted and thin. To have men devour you with their eyes when you walked into a room ...

Gina blinked away. As if she hadn't done enough damage, even looking the way she did.

Steeling herself, she closed her sliding door and curtains, and exited the bedroom to make herself something to eat. She left her notebook behind. Too much trouble to keep track of it while she cooked. And goodness knows any one of the other contestants would love to get their hands on it.

An enticing smell hit Gina before she reached the main floor. Someone was frying onions.

She entered the kitchen to find Lance hulking over the stove, stirring something in a pan with a wooden spoon.

"Smells good."

He smiled briefly, but the gesture looked false. Lance was clearly still troubled by that last set of clues. Did she appear as transparent to him as he did to her?

"What are you making?"

"Onions here." He tapped a pan with the spoon. "And burgers here." He gestured to a second pan, where two patties were cooking. "You want to make one when I'm done?"

Gina hesitated. Maybe viewers should see her eating only vegetables and fruit …

"Sure."

"There's more meat in the refrigerator. I defrosted about three pounds so we'd all have plenty."

How about that. Somebody actually doing a nice thing for the others.

Gina opened the refrigerator door and pulled out the covered plate of meat, followed by cheese, tomatoes, and lettuce. "Buns anywhere?"

"In the pantry."

She brought out a package of buns, then began forming a patty for herself.

Tension began to vibrate between her and Lance.

No doubt he wanted to know why Aaron hated her so much. And what about Lance's last clue? That man he once interviewed—testifying in a trial about a theft. Who was the victim? The defendant? How did that connect to Lance?

Twice Gina opened her mouth to ask him, then thought better of it. She had enough of an enemy in Aaron. She didn't want to make another one.

By the time Lance was eating at the counter and Gina was frying her burger, Tori, Craig, and Aaron had entered the kitchen. Still no sign of Shari. Gina would not even look at Aaron. Detestable man. She could feel the hatred roll off him. As if everything that had happened was her fault alone.

The others glanced between Aaron and her, apparently bracing for another confrontation. Aaron ignored them all. Face set and hard, he made himself a cold sandwich and sat down beside Lance. Tori hung around the center island, waiting her turn to cook meat. Craig rummaged through the freezer and pulled out a single steak. "Guess I'll have to pan fry it. No grill."

He put it on a plate and slid it into the microwave. Punched *defrost*.

No one spoke. Gina cooked, and Craig and Tori waited, and the other two ate. Gina thought of the viewers, breathlessly poised for something to happen. For one of them to snap at the other. Go for each others' throats.

One Sunday in church Gina's pastor had spoken about what a world without God would be like. No good in it. Everyone self-absorbed and deceitful. Guilty of sin yet judging only others, never themselves. That's what Gina felt right here, right now.

A life devoid of God, the pastor had continued, was just the same.

That sermon had brought Gina to her senses. Made her realize how far she'd strayed.

She flicked a look at Aaron.

Craig broke the silence. "It'll be dark before long. And still no Shari."

A shiver ran down Gina's spine. Something had to be wrong. "We should have looked for her." Now they'd have to wait until morning.

"I don't know," Tori said. "Maybe she was supposed to go out that gate. I was just looking through all my notes. When George Fry said we'd get an extra clue for winning the most votes he told us to turn on our personal camera, state our question, and then something about we would 'be given instructions on how to receive the answer.' Something like that."

Craig scratched his cheek. "Yeah, you're right. So maybe Shari was told to go somewhere past the fence to do that."

Tori nodded. "But she hasn't come back."

The microwave dinged. Craig opened the door to take out his steak.

Lance wiped grease off his fingers with a napkin. "Or she was told to go do something."

"Like what?" Craig set his steak on the counter.

"I don't know. Some task to earn the answer."

"Yeah. I'll buy that."

Gina pressed down her patty with a spatula. "But would she be gone so long?"

Craig shrugged. "Depends on what they told her to do."

"Well, it shouldn't take till after dark. That's not safe."

"But we don't know what's out there. What if, beyond all those bushes and trees, there's a little cabin? And since she went past the gate, maybe she can elect to do something else to earn back the votes she was docked. Point is, this game's been nothing but surprises from the beginning. So who knows?"

"You're right about that." Gina slid her burger from the pan onto a plate. She walked to the cabinet that held glasses—and sudden light from the backyard caught her eye. She peered out the window.

"Hey." She pointed. "That path beyond the gate just lit up. Little ground lights on each side of it."

Craig moved beside her. "Oh. That's good. Means Shari can find her way back after dark."

Gina stared at the lights. "Guess so." She *hoped* so.

"Yeah, you wait." Sarcasm tainted Aaron's voice. "Miss Love-The-Camera will be back by eight o'clock to hear who won the next round."

But what if she wasn't? A sickening thought crept into Gina's mind. What if Aaron *had* done something to Shari? Or maybe one of the other men? Everyone here hid darkness of some kind.

What were these people capable of?

Gina would have to put her guard up even more.

Chapter 15

Seven-thirty. Half an hour before the next vote winner announcement. Darkness had fallen, but the breeze filtering around Craig's closed bedroom curtains was still warm. Unseen, the ocean surged in the distance. Craig pulled the sliding door shut and locked it. He picked up his notebook and slipped into the hallway, locking the bedroom door as well. He mounted the steps—and heard voices arguing as he reached the second floor. Tori and Lance were going at it.

"... you saw Bruce again at that trial, didn't you?" Tori's tone was accusing.

Bruce. That name wasn't in Lance's clue. Craig slowed in the hall, out of sight. Listening.

"I don't have to tell you anything, Tori. So just shut up!"

Wow. Such base words from the pretentious talker.

"All those viewers out there, watching, and you don't want to say anything?" The direction of Tori's voice changed, as if she was addressing a camera. "I think he has something to hide, don't you?"

"And what about you?" Lance shot back. "Dating someone ten years younger. Does that feed your sense of superiority? You jilt him after four months or did he jilt you?"

"My personal life is no concern to you."

"Apparently it *is*. To me and all the viewers out there."

No response.

"I think *you* jilted him. Just like your husband did to you all those years ago, after you supported him through med school. It's payback time for the male persuasion, isn't that right, Tori?"

"You think you're so clever." The words sizzled.

"Indeed."

Craig heard footsteps at the bottom of the stairs. He'd soon be spotted.

"So." Tori's voice. "I'm going to ask you one more time. And remember—if you're caught in a lie ... *Did* you see Bruce at that trial?"

"*No.*"

"You didn't attend the trial?"

"No."

"Who was Bruce testifying for?"

"I don't know!"

The footsteps hit the top landing. Aaron came around the corner. He locked eyes with Craig and slowed.

"Then why was that clue even listed, Lance?"

Understanding flicked across Aaron's face. He stilled.

"I have no idea, I don't run this show! If I did, these spinning scenarios would not be happening!"

"What 'spinning scenarios?' Like clues about you that scare you to death?"

Footsteps in the great room stomped toward the door. Lance barreled through, seeing first Craig, then Aaron eavesdropping. His crimson face turned even redder. He smacked his palm against the wall and headed toward the kitchen.

Aaron and Craig looked at each other. Aaron remained poker-faced. He passed Craig without a word and went into the great room.

Craig hesitated, then followed Lance. He found the big man at the pantry, yanking out a bag of cookies. Lance ignored him. Craig leaned against the center island, watching as the man slumped onto a counter stool and ripped open the bag. The sound of his crunching filled the room. He swallowed and stuck his hand in the bag for another, then half turned toward Craig. "What are *you* lookin' at?"

"Somebody who apparently eats all the time."

Lance's mouth stopped, then chewed again. "And this erroneous observance is important to you because?"

"I'd call it Gluttony."

Lance's expression darkened. "Good for you. I'd call you Lust."

"Really."

Lance scoffed. "I've seen the way you consume Shari with your eyes. *Consumed.* Now she's missing." He drew out another cookie. "Might you have had something to do with her disappearance?"

"*You're* the one who told us she went out the back gate."

"What if I conjured that tale?"

"Did you?"

"Perhaps."

"Why?"

"To placate the women."

Craig tossed his notebook on the counter. "Not real helpful, do you think? If Shari's in trouble, we ought to be looking for her."

"Suit yourself. I'm not going anywhere."

Craig smirked. So much for the affable radio guy. "I think this show's getting to you."

"Aren't you the psychologist."

Craig looked at a camera and shook his head.

"Go ahead, Mr. Nice Guy, curry favor with the viewers. They're voting for me."

"Why would they do that?"

Lance tilted his head up toward a watching lens. "Because you desire to learn more about superficial Tori, correct? And I promised you I'd ask for a clue about her. So please log in your votes. You have twenty more minutes."

Gina entered the kitchen, catching the look on Lance's face. She slowed, glancing from him to Craig. "I was just going to get a diet soda."

Craig shrugged. "Go for it. If the lug over here doesn't bite you first."

Lance threw him a look. "As I recall, Aaron was the one she should be worried about."

At the name, Gina's chin lifted, as if she refused to be intimidated. She headed for the fridge, took out a soda, and left.

Craig picked up his notebook and turned to go. "When you get home, Mr. Radio Man, I'll bet you don't have a job anymore."

He headed for the great room, smiling.

Chapter 16

Lance waited until two minutes before eight o'clock to exit the kitchen. No use lingering in the great room with everyone else any longer than necessary. He entered the room, mouth firm, making sure to catch no one's eye. *Don't talk to me, I won't talk to you.*

Ever since the second set of clues three hours ago, Lance's nerves had felt like over-plucked strings. What must his son be thinking as he watched the show? Surely Scott wouldn't believe his father had told the producers any information about Bruce Egan. Scott had to be nearly apoplectic about now. Just like Lance.

Two more days of this. Four more sets of clues ...

Lance walked to the front of the room, near the sliding doors and assumed a wide-legged stance. No need to gather close to the monitor. He'd manage to read the announcement from where he stood. Craig was already hovering in front of the screen along with Aaron. The women kept distance.

Come on, vote for me.

Lance so wanted revenge on Tori for how she'd attacked him. If he won this round he'd ask a question about her whose answer would lay her bare.

"Here we go." Craig said.

Lance braced himself.

The monitor glowed with light, fading into the *Dream Prize* logo. Then the logo faded, replaced with text.

This round's majority of votes go to Lance Haslow.

Lance gaped at the monitor. He'd done it!

Tori turned and shot him a look to kill.

A slow smile spread across Lance's face. "Sorry, Tori the Torch. Perhaps next time."

He strode from the room.

Down in his bedroom he proceeded straight to his desk chair and smacked on the camera. The green light appeared.

"I want to know about Tori. What was the illness that plagued her after she quit her waitressing job?"

Lance sat back and waited. After a long minute words appeared on his screen. He leaned forward.

Your question has been registered. To find the answer, go through the backyard gate and follow the path about fifty yards. Take your notebook. Don't let anyone see you leave. You will not be penalized for going outside the fence. You'll come to a small shed with a door. Go inside, down the steps, and through the next door. You'll find a room with a table in the center. On that table is a monitor with your clue. Shari is there, waiting to perform a required task with you. Hurry, or she will be able to see the answer to your clue.

Lance sank back in his chair. So Craig was right. This arcane show was moving people from one venue to another.

However—a shed with descending stairs? Doubt niggled at Lance. Didn't sound too welcoming a place. And it was dark outside.

But he'd seen the path lights still burning when he was in the kitchen.

Lance hung before the monitor, weighing his decision, then reached to turn off the camera. "I must take my leave to pick up my answer. Be back with you soon."

He punched the button, and the green light faded.

Lance grabbed his notebook and hurried from the room.

Aaron's Notebook

Sunday, 8:30 p.m.

Shari #2 clue: ex roommate—Kathryn Flex. (!)
Bedroom photo of Shari and friend—Kathryn.

Brochure on Shari's desk—Sundowner Apartments. ?
Where she and K. lived? Why important?

Lance's pictures: beach and sunbathers. Lance and
young boy. Courtroom.

Lance's last clue: man he interviewed in March
testifies as witness at trial in October.

Trial = courtroom pic

Lance and boy pic—son?

Son defendant in trial? But wouldn't be a secret.

Lance's secret--??

Trial—theft of $50K. Lance guilty and someone else blamed?

Lance = Greed?

Chapter 17

She'd found the camera.

Shari slumped in the hard metal folding chair, staring at the hole in the wall across from her, near the ceiling. Behind it sat the lens. You wouldn't see it unless you were close, searching for it. She couldn't see the rest of the camera or its green light. Just the lens, staring at her, gobbling down her panic for all to see. While she'd screamed and cried and run for the grimy bathroom to throw up—the world had watched.

She wrapped her arms around her chest and shivered.

At first when she'd found the lens, Shari tried to pull herself together. She became careful of the way she moved and spoke, her facial expressions—as she always did in front of a camera. But the energy for that soon faded. Besides, it was too late. They'd seen her at her worst.

Shari's gaze lowered to the floor. She didn't know which was worse. Being filmed like that. Or not—in which case no one would even know she was here.

"Somebody please call someone in Australia to come get me," she begged—again. "We caught the boat at Perth. The trip was over an hour. Maybe you can find the boat owner who brought us. We're on a small island. The beach and house face west. We came around the south side of the island to get here."

By now in the States people had to be outraged over what *Dream Prize* was doing. FBI agents had probably raided George Fry's office and were calling Australian cops right now, telling them to send someone to the island and save her. If they could find the island.

Why had the *Dream Prize* creators done this?

They had to know they couldn't get away with it. All Shari could think at first was—publicity. Imagine the media frenzy right now. *Everyone* would be watching the show. Everyone would be talking about it online.

Shari licked her lips, envisioning the videos of her going out across Facebook. The millions of hits. People would feel sorry for her. Come to think of it, she would be famous. When she walked into her next audition, people would know her. They might choose her for the part because of her celebrity.

Maybe she could still be a star.

Was *this* how the show planned to make good on her dream prize when she won? What a sick way to do it.

Still, it tugged at the hope within her.

Shari leaned over and picked up her notebook, lying on the floor at her feet. In the dim light she had to hold it close to read her own writing. She tried to focus on the second set of clues, but her mind wouldn't settle. How could she concentrate on others while trapped *here*? Whenever she got back to her bedroom—feeling like she'd escaped a death sentence—she'd study her notes. Piece together what she could.

Shari tossed her notebook down. It fell with a light *thud* on the concrete. She leaned over and covered her face with her hands.

A *click* sounded to her right. Shari jerked up.

Lance stepped through the door.

What?

Shari rammed out of her chair. "Don't *close it*!"

Lance blinked, then turned to grab the knob, dropping his notebook. The door banged shut.

"*Nnnno!*" Shari ran past Lance and yanked on the handle. It wouldn't move. She pushed and kicked the door, fresh tears welling in her eyes, knowing, *knowing* it wouldn't work.

"What are you *doing*?"

Shari barely heard Lance's words. She pulled her hands away from the knob, then slowly melted forward to lean her forehead against the door. She let out a sob.

"Shari!"

She twisted toward Lance. "*Why'd* you let it close? Are you *stupid*?"

He gaped at her. "I was told to come here to receive my clue."

Shari let out a laugh so dark it scared her. "Oh, right. Let me guess. It'll come on this monitor."

Lance eyed her, uncomprehending. He pivoted toward the screen on the table. It was dark.

"Nothing will happen, Lance." Shari's voice sounded dead. "They got me in here with the same thing. Now they've tricked you."

"What?"

"We're *trapped*, don't you get it? Stuck in here."

"That's impossible."

"Try the door."

Lance stepped to the door and fought to twist the knob. It wouldn't move. He jerked and pulled. Still nothing.

He swung around to face Shari. "Why are we locked in here? Until when?"

Shari laughed again, deep in her throat. "Like *I* know." She stumbled toward the nearest chair and fell into it.

Lance just kept standing there, like a big idiot. "You telling me there's no way out of here?"

"Try the door again if you want."

He wiped his forehead. "Have you been in here since you went through the fence gate?"

Shari's head snapped up. "How do *you* know I went through the gate?"

Lance's mouth closed, like he'd said something he shouldn't.

Shari pushed to her feet. "How do you *know?*"

"I witnessed the act."

She barged up to him and shoved him in the chest. The big lug didn't even move. "You *saw* me? Why didn't you come looking for me?"

"I didn't know where you were."

"You knew I was *missing!* For over six hours now." She pushed him again. "And you didn't even care?"

Lance caught her arm and held on—hard. "Back off."

Shari wrenched away. "Why didn't you come?"

"We didn't know where you were. We talked about it—and decided you'd been commanded to go through the gate in order to earn your clue." Lance spread his hands. "Which apparently was true."

"You think I'd choose to be gone that long? After dark?" Shari jabbed a finger in the air. "You all just don't care. One less person to worry about losing to. Especially since it was clear I'd *win.*"

"In your dreams, as the hoi polloi would say." Lance strode over to swipe his notebook off the floor.

Who?

Shari's eyes cut to her own notebook, lying near a chair. Turn her back, and he might just steal it. She snatched it up.

Lance checked the monitor again.

"You won't find your clue, now or ever." Shari stuck the notebook under her arm.

Disgust creased Lance's face. "This is insanity."

"And that's not all. See over there?" Shari pointed to the far wall. "That little hole? That's the camera."

Lance ogled it, chin thrust out. Then made his way over for a closer look.

"Great shot up your nose for the viewers."

"I don't see a green light."

"You can be sure it's on. The camera's obviously in some kind of box behind the wall."

Lance turned toward her. "Then people know we're here."

"Clever, Sherlock."

"So they can't keep us locked up. That's kidnapping."

"Nobody made us come here."

"But they're not letting us *go*. That's false imprisonment."

Well, didn't he know so much.

Shari's legs suddenly felt weak. She sat down hard.

Lance spotted the opening to the bathroom across from him. He went over to investigate. Shari heard him turn on the sink faucet. He reappeared, looked around, and headed for the refrigerator. Opened it. "Wonderful. Water bottles and food to last me an hour."

"You'd better not eat any of that food! We have to divide it. Who knows how long we'll be down here."

Lance closed the refrigerator door. He hesitated, then walked over to the table to check the monitor again.

Guy wouldn't learn.

He tossed his notebook on the table. "Somebody else will come. Tomorrow after two o'clock, when the next vote winner is announced. It's a long time away, but at least ..."

"Great, that'll make three of us. A real party."

"But we can ready ourselves. When the next victim enters, we'll catch the door before it closes."

Relief shot through Shari, then fizzled. She pictured herself coming through the first door hours earlier, how it had closed on its own.

"Won't matter. You can be sure the top door locks automatically, just like this one. We'll still be trapped."

"At least we'll be closer to freedom. If we bang on that door, someone may hear."

Shari closed her eyes, picturing how far the shed door was beyond the backyard gate. The gate that no one would go near. "They won't hear us. It's a thick door."

Lance started to pace the room. "Has to be something we can do."

Six hours, Shari thought. She was six hours ahead of him, of his schemes for breaking out of here. Plenty of time for her own wild plans to die. In time his would die too. There would be no escape on their own, she knew that.

"We'll get out of here only when someone rescues us."

Lance pulled to a halt. He swiveled and pointed to the camera. "You cannot get away with this, George Fry! I will *sue* you and your network!"

"Yeah, well, get in line." Shari rubbed her forehead.

"There was nothing in our contract about being treated like this."

"Yeah, but we did have to agree not to hold the show liable for anything, right?" Shari had remembered that fact around hour number three. "And I wasn't dumb about that contract. I even paid a media lawyer to look over it before I signed. He said that liability clause was standard for a reality show."

"This is different, though. This is *criminal*." Lance punched the air and went back to pacing like a big gorilla.

All the commotion was only making Shari's anxiety rise. She closed her eyes, but the *thomp-thomp* of Lance's flip flops grated her ears. "Would you stop! You're driving me crazy."

The man ignored her and kept walking.

"Lance! *Stop!*"

"Shut up!" His face turned crimson. "I'm trying to think."

"How about thinking in silence!"

He kept pacing. Moron. Shari put her hands over her ears.

Lance wouldn't quit.

Fine then. Shari jumped up and trotted to the center table. Snatched up his notebook.

"Hey!" He skidded toward her and grabbed the spine of the book. Shari held on.

"Let go!"

She yanked the notebook out of his hands. Shoved it behind her back.

"Give it to me!" Lance pushed to get around her, but she jerked away. He moved toward it again.

Another pivot.

Lance grabbed her by the throat.

Shari stilled, her eyes widening. His thumb pressed against her larynx.

"Drop it."

His thumb was sinking deeper. Shari couldn't breathe. Terror flooded her. This man was *big*. She was stuck down here with him, and he could do anything to her …

She let go of the notebook. It tumbled over her foot and hit the floor.

Lance hung on to her for a second longer, then shoved her away. She stumbled backward, choking.

He raised a finger and pointed at her. "You do *not* want to push me right now."

Shari encircled her throbbing neck with her hands and backed up. She couldn't get far enough away from this lunatic. When she bumped into a chair she collapsed into it, shaking.

Lance glared at her, then walked with taunting purpose to the refrigerator and pulled out the one small packet of salami.

Chapter 18

Tori sat at a table on the deck off the great room, looking over her notebook. Lights hanging from the deck's roof were plenty bright for reading. But the words still blurred. Tori had hardly slept the night before. And this interminable day had taken its toll. She longed for bed, but it was too early. And even there—would she actually sleep? She'd accomplished so little since she'd gotten here. Once she'd made her notes after the second set of clues, she hadn't figured out any more of the puzzle.

And only two more days to work at it.

In the distance the ocean surged. Below the deck a warm breeze *shooshed* through leaves. Inside the house all was quiet, but uneasiness and stress still roiled in every corner. Looking over her shoulder, Tori could see Craig sitting in the great room alone, writing in his notebook. The others were nowhere in sight.

Still no sign of Shari.

Tori closed her eyes and pulled in a long breath.

Footsteps sounded from inside. Tori glanced up to see Aaron crossing the great room, heading toward her.

Wonderful.

He slid open the screen door and stepped onto the deck. Looked Tori over and nodded.

"Hi." She didn't smile.

This guy was the quintessential computer programmer. Tori saw many of them in her own company. Smart. Logical thinkers. Detail oriented and completely fixated when it came to solving a problem.

Aaron indicated a chair at Tori's table. "May I?"

What did he want? She nodded.

He took a seat, laying his notebook on the table. "I have a proposition for you." He kept his voice low.

Tori glanced at Craig. He was watching them from his seat on the sofa, too far away to hear.

"Yes?"

"I give you a piece of information, you give me one."

So. Negotiations. Tori was good at this. She folded her arms and leaned back. "Depends on the information."

Aaron tapped his notebook. "I came up the stairs today and heard you and Lance arguing. Sounded like you were asking about that guy testifying in the trial. Earlier, when we got the second list of clues, you also argued. You mentioned the name Bruce."

Tori suppressed a wince. Had she really said that name in front of everybody? She'd have to be more careful with the information she gleaned. "Well, haven't you been all ears."

Aaron shrugged.

"I'm surprised you heard anything after the clues, given how focused you were on tearing Gina apart."

No response. What a poker player.

"So what do you want, Aaron? You haven't told me anything I don't know."

"Who was the defendant in that trial, and who did Bruce testify for—defense or prosecution?"

Neither of which answer Tori knew. "And what information do I get in return?"

"I know the three photographs hanging in Shari's bedroom."

Tori's eyebrows rose. "You were in Shari's *room?*"

A nod.

That sure hadn't taken long. "Well, aren't you the bad boy, Aaron Wang."

He laced his long fingers, eyeing Tori coolly.

"You have any idea where Shari is?"

"No."

Was he lying? "Clearly you've been more familiar with her than anyone else."

"I don't know where she is. Do you want to accept my proposal or not?"

"I'd want different information."

Aaron lifted a hand —*what?*

"What did Gina do to your parents?"

Aaron stiffened. "No."

"Then we don't have a deal."

His eyes narrowed.

"Why won't you tell me that?"

He studied Tori with a hard expression, as if weighing his decision. His eyes flicked toward the deck's camera and back.

Interesting. Was he protecting his parents?

Tori pulled her pen from its loop in her notebook. Ripped out a sheet of paper and wrote: *You don't want the world to hear?* She slid the paper toward Aaron, shielding the words from the camera lens.

He read, looked up and nodded.

Tori's voice dropped to a whisper. "You can write the answer. Then destroy the piece of paper."

"No."

She replaced her pen. "Then we're done here."

Aaron glowered at her, then crumpled her note with one hand. He pushed back his chair and stood, stuffing the paper in his pocket.

"You may be betting on the wrong thing, regarding your parents." Tori looked up at him. "For all you know the answer to my question may be in the next clue about you."

The corners of Aaron's mouth pulled in. He strode across the deck and yanked open the screen door, slamming it closed behind him.

Tori slid out her pen and leaned over her notebook.

Aaron slept with Shari—before 2:00, when she disappeared!
Aaron: ~~*Wrath*~~*. Lust?*

DREAM PRIZE

Day Two

Monday, March 7

Chapter 19

Two a.m.

Aaron lay in bed, staring at the ceiling. No moonlight in his room. His sliding door was open a crack, the curtains closed. Dark stillness. Ocean surge. Should lull him to sleep.

He was too wired.

Clues. Faces. Conversations. Like snakes in his mind. Gina—disgusting liar. Lance—white-faced after second clues. Tori—know-it-all. Craig—pretended calm. What was he hiding?

Shari. Where *was* she?

After eight o'clock Aaron had seen only Tori and Craig before going to his room. Gina? Probably in her bedroom, plotting. Lance? Same thing.

Aaron had written in his notebook past midnight. Trying to sort out details. He only went 'round and 'round. This puzzle was not like solving a glitch in software. With that, he could try one thing, test it. If it didn't work, try something else. Here he saw little progress.

How to prove his suspicions?

Did Tori really think he'd slept with Shari? *That* would be funny.

The misperception did give Aaron an idea. If he couldn't find answers to his questions, he could plant wrong answers in others' minds. Not lie. Just drop hints. Breadcrumbs down the wrong path. Play defense *and* offense.

Gina's face hovered in Aaron's brain. He hated her. She'd caused his mother hurt. She would pay.

Why had this show brought them together?

Were other contestants linked?

Why those two clues about himself?

The clue about his father brought out his connection to Gina. But the convention clue?

It put him in L.A. Where he'd gone to dinner at the restaurant …

What if future clues led to what happened after he left the restaurant?

They couldn't lead there. No one else knew that.

So why—

A *ping* sounded from the desk.

What? Aaron squinted into the darkness.

Light played across his monitor.

He sat up and threw off the covers. Went over to the desk.

The *Dream Prize* logo appeared on his screen.

A surprise set of clues coming? Dread and anticipation swirled through Aaron. He flicked on the desk lamp and pulled the pen from his notebook.

The show's logo disappeared. Text filled the monitor.

Aaron, as runner-up winner of the last count of votes, you have the opportunity to earn an extra clue of your choice. But you must act now. To pick up your clue, go through the backyard gate and follow the

path about fifty yards. Take your notebook. Do not let anyone hear you leave. You will not be penalized for going outside the fence. You'll come to a small shed with a door. Go inside, down the steps, and through the next door, closing it immediately. You'll find a room with a table in the center. On that table is a camera and monitor which you can use to state your desired clue and receive the answer. Shari is there, waiting to perform a required task with you. If you do not speak into the camera in that room within the next fifteen minutes, the opportunity for an additional clue will transfer to Shari.

Aaron read the words. Read them again.

So that's where Shari was.

Fifteen minutes.

Here was his chance to find out about Lance and that guy at the trial. Bruce.

Aaron tossed down his pen. Swept his shorts and T shirt off the floor. He threw them on, gathered up his notebook, pen, and room key. He started to leave, then remembered the sliding glass door. He closed and locked it.

Aaron slipped out of his bedroom, locked the door, and hurried down the hall.

Chapter 20

Seven-fifteen in the morning.

Gina had woken up early after a fitful night's sleep. Her muscles were tight, her head aching. She downed two aspirin, then took a shower and put on her make-up. Slipped into thin blue flowing pants and a matching top. Desperate prayers filtered through the back of her mind. *Help me get through this day, Jesus. Please.* Again, she was hit by her lack of prayer about coming on this show. She should have started praying the day she'd received the email inviting her to audition. If she had asked for God's direction, He'd have warned her. Somehow. She wouldn't be here right now. Her knees wouldn't be knocking over the thought of the next set of clues.

Help me, please! I don't want to keep lying.

Gina picked up her notebook and dragged herself up the stairs for breakfast. She entered an empty kitchen— and breathed a sigh of relief.

In all four corners of the room, the camera lights flicked from red to green.

Gina tried to gather her wits, imagining the millions of eyes on her. Watching, gauging her every move and expression. Her nerves tingled. She longed to run back down the stairs and hide in her room.

She took a deep breath and forced a tight smile. Gazed up at the nearest camera. "Good morning. Nothing much happening here except—trying to decide what to eat."

Truth was, Gina longed for eggs and bacon and toast. But that would take so long to make, and what if Aaron showed up? She didn't dare be alone in a room with him.

She grabbed milk and a box of cereal. A bowl and spoon. Sat down at the counter and began to eat.

A minute later footsteps sounded behind her. She jerked her head around.

Craig.

She blew out air. "Oh. Hi."

He studied her. "You all right?"

Oh, yeah, she was great. "I'm fine. Have you seen Shari?" Anything to get his focus off her.

"No. You?"

"No. Wonder if she's back. I haven't seen Lance or Aaron yet either. Or Tori. Maybe they're all in their rooms."

Craig placed his notebook on the center island. "Probably. Or on the beach."

He gave Gina another once-over. "The way you jumped when I came in. Were you afraid I was Aaron?"

She hesitated. "Yeah."

"I'll bet. So what did you do to his parents?"

Gina sighed. "Nothing."

"You did something."

"I sold them a house."

"Was it a bad deal? Full of termites?"

"*No.* And I don't want to talk anymore about it."

"That's why we're here—to find out about each other. Remember?"

"Well, maybe I don't want to play anymore."

"Fine, then, give me your notebook and tell me everything you know. You can hide in your room for the next two days."

Gina smacked her spoon on the counter. "Why don't you just leave me alone? All I want to do is eat breakfast in peace."

Craig shrugged and headed for the refrigerator.

The guy acted so cool and sure of himself. When Gina first saw him she'd found his face friendly-looking. He'd *acted* friendly. This game was changing him.

She pushed her half-eaten bowl of cereal away. "What did *you* do?"

"To who?"

"Anybody."

"What kind of a question is that?"

"All right, to the accountant you hired in 2013? The one your last clue was about?"

Craig pulled a carton of eggs and package of sausage from the fridge. Set them down by the stove.

"You gonna answer my question?"

"I hired him. He worked for me. End of story."

"Worked?" Gina raised her eyebrows. "Meaning he doesn't anymore?"

Craig flicked a look at her, as if he'd let something slip. "No."

"Why? You fire him?"

"No."

"Why then?"

Craig turned his back on Gina and looked up at a camera. "I'm just trying to fix my breakfast here, and look how she's going at me. You know why she's doing it? She's trying to get attention away from *herself*. As in — *what* did she do to Aaron's parents?" Craig pointed at the lens. "And if you're as curious about that as I am, vote for me this morning. If I win the votes at two o'clock, I'll ask for the answer."

Heat spritzed through Gina's limbs. This was never going to let up. First Aaron, now Craig. And she faced another set of clues in half an hour. What if it was *the* clue? What if it answered Craig's question?

Craig put butter into a pan and turned on the burner beneath it. He glanced toward the hall. "Last night Aaron and Tori were talking out on the deck. Pretty intense conversation. They thought I couldn't hear, but I could. He told Tori what you did to his parents."

Gina's heart stilled. If that was true, the cameras out there had picked it up. Now the world knew. *Ben* knew. Her throat closed up.

She heard herself laugh, high and off key. "You're lying. Because I didn't do anything."

"That's not what he said."

"Then *he's* lying."

Craig smirked at her. "Right."

Gina pushed off her stool. On someone else's legs, she walked her dirty bowl and spoon to the dishwasher. Stuck them inside. Was Craig lying? *Was* he? If he was telling the truth, she should talk into her own bedroom camera. Try to convince everyone out there—*Ben*—that Aaron had made it all up. But if Craig was lying and she started babbling into the camera for no reason, she could do herself a lot of harm.

Back at the eating counter, Gina grabbed her notebook and turned to leave. She needed to get out of there. She needed to *think*. No way could she get through the next set of clues in this condition.

"Nice talking to you." Craig's tone mocked.

Gina raised her chin and stalked from the kitchen.

Chapter 21

Craig entered the great room ten minutes before nine o'clock, carrying his notebook. His pulse zinged in anticipation of the next clues. Another day and a half of this craziness, of being in the same house with these detestable people. If he could just manage until Tuesday afternoon ...

He forced his mind away from his fears—and on to Gina and their conversation in the kitchen. Now that was a better topic. Craig managed a chuckle. He'd gotten to her, all right. Left Gina wondering which way was up. She did a mighty poor job of hiding her emotions. Clearly she didn't know whether to believe him or not. Play his cards right, and he'd force her to admit what she'd done—in front of the cameras. Nothing like a guilty conscience to get a person chattering when they should keep their mouth shut.

Craig wandered over to the sliding door and gazed at the ocean, one finger tapping his thigh.

The sound of someone approaching made him turn. It was Tori, looking like she'd barely slept. Her makeup was perfect, and her cream colored silk beach slacks and top looked expensive. But Craig saw the bags under her eyes.

She glanced at him, then flicked her eyes away. Interesting.

"Good morning." Craig kept his voice light.

"Hi." She still wouldn't look at him.

"You don't look too happy."

Tori positioned herself in front of the monitor.

Perfect time to shake another tree and see what fell.

Craig opened his notebook and ran his finger down the last set of clues. "So you dated some guy ten years younger than yourself. When was it—three years ago?"

Tori lifted a shoulder.

"Why's that so important?"

"Ask George Fry."

Craig smiled. "He just might be telling us in a minute."

Tori turned toward Craig, her mouth pinched. "And what's so important about you hiring an accountant?"

Craig eyed her. "Come to think of it, that was three years ago, too."

She shook her head—*so?*

Craig looked back to his notebook. "Know what? The clues about Gina and Aaron were also in 2013. And those two are connected. Plus, Aaron seemed so convinced there were more connections." Craig frowned at Tori. "Is there some link between your clue and mine?"

"Why would there be?"

"You tell me."

"I *can't*, because there isn't one."

"You sure?"

"Not that I know of."

Craig raised his chin and regarded her. She seemed to shrivel under his gaze. "Hm."

Gina came into the room, looking like a mouse the cat dragged in. She glanced from Craig to Tori. "Where's everybody else?"

Craig checked the clock on the wall. One minute before nine. "Whoa, it's almost time. They should be here."

"I haven't seen any sign of them this morning," Tori said. "Shari may still be gone. Which is ... I don't know what to think about that."

"What if they're *all* gone?" Gina's eyes rounded.

"That's ... no." Tori shook her head. "They'll be here."

Craig watched emotions flit over Gina's face, as if she couldn't decide which would be worse—Aaron showing up, or more people missing.

The clock's minute hand jerked to nine. Craig drew in a breath. "It's time."

The monitor lit up.

DREAM PRIZE

Monday 9 a.m.

On the weekend *Gina's* husband was out of town in July 2013, she went to dinner with a former client at the five-star restaurant, Trancet, in L.A.

~~~

In October 2013 the accountant *Craig* had hired in June fell into deep depression.

~~~

On January 8, 2014, on his last night in L.A. for the convention, *Aaron* went to dinner with his mother.

~~~

In early June 2012, *Shari's* roommate at the time, Kathryn Flex, lost her lead role in *Last Bend*.

~~~

On November 8, 2012, the defendant for the trial in which *Lance's* interviewee had testified for the prosecution was convicted.

~~~

In early October 2013, *Tori* abruptly ended her relationship with the younger man she'd been dating and began seeing another younger man.

Chapter 22

Tori's heart slammed against her ribs as the clues appeared. Her fingers gripped the pen poised above her notebook.

Easy. Breathe.

Text filled the screen. Tori steeled herself. If they told about her suicide attempts after her husband left her years ago, or the following months in the mental ward, Tori could kiss her CEO dreams goodbye. No matter that she'd pulled herself up, had proven herself. No matter that she was now strong and the one in control. No board would overlook the depths to which she'd sunk when the going got too tough.

Her eyes dropped to her clue at the end.

In early October 2013 Tori abruptly ended her relationship with the younger man she'd been dating and began seeing another younger man.

Air blew from Tori's mouth.

Not too bad. Could have been worse. But—why all this about her personal life? Yes, she fell in and out of

love with men. And so what if they tended to be younger?
Lots of women dated younger men these days.

Tori, write!

She pushed her thoughts aside and started scribbling.

The second one—Craig's clue about his accountant—
stopped her hand. Nate, in depression? And right after
she'd broken off with him. Was it because of *her*? She'd
never spoken to him again since that night.

Guilt panged through Tori. Had she made Nate as
miserable as her husband had made her when he dumped
her for a younger woman?

Surely not. She and Nate had been seeing each other
for just a few months—and even then only on weekends.
Tori had been Merill's wife and had spent years working
to put him through med school. She'd given her *life* to the
man.

Tori shook her head and kept writing. Her hand
moved automatically, her mind focused on getting down
every word.

Not until she finished did she realize Lance, Aaron,
and Shari had never appeared.

No, no. This was ...

What was happening?

Gina looked up from her writing and locked eyes with
Tori. The realtor was visibly shaking, her face pale. Tori
glanced at her notebook, re-reading Gina's clue.

The meaning registered in her brain.

Gina's husband, out of town—that had to be
significant—and Gina out to dinner with a former client.

Aaron's *father*?

Tori turned back to Gina, who stared at her like a
deer in headlights.

"Where's Aaron, Gina?" Accusation hardened Tori's
voice. Had this women had an *affair* on her husband?
Just like Tori's husband had done to her?

"How should I know?"

"It would sure be convenient for you if he was gone."

Gina looked away. Her chest rose and fell with her breathing.

"Leave her alone." Craig moved close to Tori, his jaw tight.

Tori drew her head back. "What's *your* problem?"

Craig glared at her. "I get it now. The connection. It *was* you, wasn't it. Who sent my employee—my good friend—into that nosedive."

Gina watched them blankly, as if still too focused on her own problems to comprehend.

"Are you crazy? I don't even live near you or your foundation."

"No. But I'll bet you travel a lot for your company. You came to Southern California, didn't you? Met him there."

What to say? Tori pictured all the rapt viewers, watching. Ogling. What would her employees at Serros think? What right did *Dream Prize* have to tell them about her private life?

"You *knew* this, Tori!" Craig's face flushed. "You had to have realized it after the second clues mentioned my accountant. Unless you just sleep with men and don't even ask what they do for a living!"

Tori slapped Craig. The *crack* sounded through the room.

Craig's head rebounded. He shot out his arm and caught her by the wrist. She dropped her notebook.

"Let me go!" The words gritted through Tori's teeth.

"It was him, wasn't it. Tell me. You told him you loved him, then dropped him like dirt. He fell into a depression he never came out of."

"Let. Me. *Go.*"

Craig gripped her harder. "*Tell* me."

Tori struggled to free herself. His fingers dug deeper into her skin.

"I'm not letting you go until you admit it."

Tori aimed a kick at Craig's shin. He jerked his leg away.

"Stop!" Gina threw down her notebook, her voice wavering. "Just stop, both of you."

"They already know, Tori." Craig gestured with his chin toward a camera. His cheek was beet red. "They see the truth all over your face. You lie—you lose votes. So tell me. It was Nate, wasn't it."

"Get off me!" Tori fought to wrench away.

Craig caught her other arm and backed her up to the table. His breath was hot on her face. "Say it."

"How *dare* you attack me! I will have you arrested when we get home!"

"You do that."

Tori struggled harder, but she couldn't break free. She had nowhere to go, no way to make Craig stop. After she'd vowed *no* man would ever mistreat her again.

She spit in Craig's face.

Rage flattened his forehead. He yanked her away from the table, then pushed her hard. Tori stumbled backward and crashed into a couch. Her legs gave out. She fell to the floor.

Craig stalked over and hulked above Tori, right hand curling and uncurling. "You think you're really something, don't you." The words dropped like stones. "You're *nothing*. You just use people. Use men up and throw them away, like they're your playthings. Nate was a good man. You *ruined* his life."

Tori shoved to her feet. She faced Craig, breathing hard, rage coursing through her veins. When she spoke her voice was low, shaking. "You don't know anything about me. You *cannot* judge me."

Gina laughed crazily. "What are you talking about—this whole *show* is about judging!"

The hysterical words rattled Tori's ears. Gina sounded almost unhinged. They were *all* coming apart at the seams.

Tori took a step backward, away from Craig. She pointed a finger at his chest. "You got your little scene, is that what you wanted? Play the bad boy and win some low-life votes? Good for you. Now don't you dare come near me again."

He laughed with disdain. "I don't want to be anywhere *near* you."

Well, they agreed on something. Tori grabbed her notebook off the floor.

"Where's Aaron and Lance?" Gina's voice sounded ragged. "They're gone now, too, just like Shari. Something's happened to all of them, I'm telling you. Before you know it, one of *us* will vanish." She tilted her head up toward a camera. "What are you doing to us? Do you think this is *funny*?"

"Wherever they are, they're safe." Craig's cheek was still crimson. He straightened his shoulders, trying to reassemble himself.

"You don't *know* that!"

"No, I don't. But I'd bet it. This show just wants to keep us off balance. Each of them went somewhere to do something specific. Maybe one of us will get some secret command next."

Gina shook her head hard. "I'm not going anywhere! This show is nothing but lies. They tricked us to get us here. Now they're tricking us every *moment*." She waved her hand at Craig. "Look at the way you two were fighting. Don't you think they *loved* that? And how Aaron came after me yesterday. The clues are set-ups."

But they were also true, Tori thought. Craig's and her clues had shown their connection. Same with Gina and Aaron. And if Tori was right about what Gina had done, a pattern was becoming clear. Sexual relationships.

But that didn't fit Lance's clues. Or Shari's. Or shed light on Aaron's or Craig's secret ...

And the biggest question of all—how did the creators of the show know these things?

Dizziness washed over Tori. None of this made any sense. She tottered to the nearest armchair and sank down. Laid her notebook in her lap.

Craig lasered Tori with his eyes. He made a disgusted sound in his throat, picked up his notebook, and strode from the room.

Good riddance.

Gina leaned weakly against the center table. "I want to just smash that thing." She made a face at the monitor.

Tori focused on the floor. She should have eaten breakfast. No wonder she felt so weak. At least her mind was clearing after that unprovoked assault. And she saw an opportunity.

"Come sit down, Gina." She spoke like a kind boss to a disheartened employee.

Gina hesitated, then made her way over to the opposite couch and fell into it with a sigh.

A long silence followed. Tori let Gina wallow in it. When her dizziness fully passed, Tori straightened.

Gina watched her. "You okay?"

"Just got woozy for a minute. I need to go eat something soon." Tori smiled.

"You probably should." Gina sounded lost, as if she had no idea what to do next.

Tori ripped a piece of paper from her notebook and wrote. *You had an affair with Aaron's father, didn't you.* She folded it and leaned forward, offering the note to Gina.

The realtor frowned, then took it. Unfolded it and read the words.

She stiffened and flicked a hard glance at Tori. "I don't know what you're talking about."

"Yes, you do. It's okay. I get it."

Talk about a *lie*. Even saying those words made Tori want to spit again.

Emotions skimmed across Gina's face. Self-defense ... fear ... defeat. She looked away at nothing.

Bingo.

Cheater. Slut. Tori's empty stomach turned sour. Did Aaron's mother know? Did Gina's husband? Tori knew all too well how they would feel if they found out.

Aaron wasn't Lust after all. This immoral woman was. Tori would tell the world exactly that at the end of the show. But she wouldn't say why she believed it, in case the abused spouses weren't aware. Tori would not be the conduit for their pain.

She pushed to her feet. Gina was Lust, no doubt about it. One deadly sin down, five more to go. Four, actually, because Tori wasn't one of them.

She had no more need of quaking Gina. In fact Tori couldn't even stand to be near the scarlet woman. Gina Corrales deserved all the angst she felt and more. She could rot in hell.

Tori turned on her heel and strode from the room.

Chapter 23

Lance guzzled his second bottled water of the morning, then crushed the thin plastic in his fingers. The *crackle* echoed off the concrete block walls.

"Stop it!" Shari smacked her hands over her ears. She was leaning against the opposite wall, jittery and bubbling with impatience. "I *hate* that sound!"

Lance tossed the bottle down, gloating at Shari as it snapped and popped all the more in revengeful crepitation. She'd done nothing but ride his nerves ever since he'd gotten locked in this awful bunker. He could take no more of this abuse.

Aaron ignored them both, sprawled and scowling in a chair with his legs apart. One foot jiggled. In the middle of the night he'd startled them out of staccatoed sleep, their heads lolling as they tilted uncomfortably in their folding chairs. Suddenly the door clicked and slammed — and there stood Aaron, gunning and anxious for an extra clue. Said he'd just received a special message on his bedroom monitor. At two o'clock in the morning. The twists in this show never ceased.

It took Aaron over an hour to accept the fact that he'd been hoodwinked. Even then he'd paced the room the rest of the night, energy crackling from him more than the bottle Lance had just demolished.

Lance eyed the refrigerator. He was exhausted and grungy and starved. He'd already eaten half the food, and that didn't begin to fill his stomach.

"Don't you *dare* eat any more," Shari spat. "You're not the only one in here who needs food."

"I'll eat what I want! Who's to stop me?"

Shari stomped toward him, a fly razzing a giant. Such sudden courage. "Aaron and I both will. We'll beat you to a pulp if we have to!"

"You think you own this place just because you were naive enough to be caught here first?"

Shari's mouth opened, then closed. She punched a fist in the air, then retreated to a chair and heaved herself into it, glowering at Lance. Not picture perfect anymore, was she. Little miss actress. Her mascara was smeared and her hair a veritable rat's nest. Apparently she was past caring.

Not that Lance could judge her for that. This show had come down to mere survival.

For a short time during the long night—before Aaron showed up—Lance and Shari had actually managed to talk a little. She'd told him of having to leave Hollywood and return home to nurse her mother. How that had hurt her career. And that she'd returned to Hollywood as soon as she could. Lance thought she'd been telling the truth. But likely her story had been more for the watching audience's benefit than for his.

Foot still jiggling, Aaron looked at his watch. He bent over to pick his notebook off the floor, then pulled to his feet.

The action bounced Lance's attention away from Shari and his hunger. He checked his own watch. Nineteen minutes after nine. If the show proceeded as before, according to Shari, the third set of clues would soon appear. Not that Lance was anxious to see what was next revealed about him and Bruce. The very thought shot fear through his loins. But to *not* know—that would be worse.

Why was the show revealing these things? And how did they *know?* Someone must have spent a lot of money on private investigators to gather the information. But who had talked in the first place, to even raise a suspicion? Bruce? Lance hadn't seen him in over three years. That had been purposeful—cut all ties. Maybe he should have kept watch on the man. You never knew what a drug addict would do.

Anger knocked through Lance. Somehow, some way, the producers of this show would *pay.* He shook a finger at the nearly invisible camera lens. "You're supposed to give us our clues. So do it! You trap us in here like animals, you can at least tell us what you're telling the others in the house."

"Yeah, right." Shari waved a hand. "Like this show is fair about *anything*. I'm still going to sue everybody involved when I get home."

Aaron threw her a look. "You talk like that, they just might leave you here." He sounded like he hoped they would.

That made two of them.

"They *have* to let us out Tuesday afternoon," Shari shot back. "You know they do."

A day and a half to go. The three of them just might kill each other before then.

The monitor pinged.

Lance grabbed his notebook and hurried over to the table. Shari and Aaron crowded beside him.

The *Dream Prize* logo appeared. Dread flushed through Lance's veins. *Here we go again.*

Maybe, just maybe they'd lay off the Bruce story …

The logo faded and clues filled the page. Lance's gaze skipped down to number four—his clue. The trial again. Bruce testifying for the prosecution. The defendant convicted.

Lance's knees went weak. Lay off, nothing. This wouldn't stop. It was *not going to stop*. Three more sets of clues left. By that time the world would know it all. His life, Scott's life, would be over.

Shari inhaled sharply. Lance could feel anger rolling from Aaron.

Somehow Lance forced his fingers to jot down the clues. Vaguely he registered Shari and Aaron writing, too.

When Lance was done he stumbled to a chair and sat down. He needed air. It was hot in here. And so dim. And food was running out. What would they *do*? Lance ran a finger under his T-shirt collar, stretching the fabric away from his skin. Sweat rolled down his back. Was Bruce watching the show? What was he thinking? Would he do something stupid? What was *Scott* thinking?

Shari leaned against the table and hacked into jagged sobs. Aaron grabbed a folding chair and shoved it against the wall. Then flipped it around and sat down hard, facing the concrete, his back to Lance. Furiously, he began to write in his notebook.

Lance couldn't concentrate on the clues. At this point what difference would it make if they guessed each others' sins? What did it even matter who won? Their lives would be ruined in the process.

Was that what *Dream Prize* had wanted all along?

Aaron's Notebook

Monday, 9:30 a.m. After Clues #3.

Gina: July 2013-Gina/former client-Trancet Restaurant. Has to be my father. First time together?

** Gina—Lust.

Me: January 8, 2014-dinner with mother in L.A. !!!

Gina → Father → me, Jan. 8 dinner with mother → next clue—what came after?

Two Oct. 2013 clues: Tori broke up with guy, Craig's accountant depressed. Connection? Same guy?

Two people connected—me/Gina. Craig/Tori connected (?) If so—Lance/Shari connected?

Chapter 24

Shortly before noon, Gina wandered around the great room, clutching her notebook. Feeling adrift. She might as well be a lost boat at sea. Actually, that would be better. No cameras.

She glanced at the nearest lens peering down at her.

That last clue! Her dinner at Trancet Restaurant. Her first date with Shan. How had they *known*? Why were they *doing* this?

By the time the last three clues were given, would it all be spelled out? What would she *do*? Her marriage would be ruined.

And three people were still missing.

Would someone come in the night and drag her away, too?

Maybe they were off doing something they'd been told to do, as Craig had guessed. But every hour they were gone made it harder for Gina to believe that. Just thinking about it now gave her the shivers. And the people *in* the house weren't much better. Craig and Tori were staying far away from each other. If one entered some room, the other one left. Tori didn't seem to want any more to do with Gina, either. That left only Craig to talk to, but no thanks. Not after the way he'd treated her in the kitchen that morning. Not to mention how he'd flat out attacked Tori.

Gina pictured the scene and shuddered. Before that she'd thought Aaron must be the deadly sin of Wrath. But even *he* hadn't pushed her to the floor, like Craig had pushed Tori.

So Craig was Wrath. Aaron was ... Pride? He sure acted like he was better than everyone else. But Shari looked a lot like Pride, too.

Lance ate a lot. He'd make the best Gluttony. And what was this about Tori, bouncing from one younger man to another? Maybe she was Lust.

Emberly. From somewhere in the depths of Gina's brain Craig's last name surfaced. *Emberly.*

Wait. Hadn't she heard that name before?

Gina stared across the room, trying to remember. The answer wouldn't come.

She fell onto the nearest couch with a sigh. What was the point of all this? She'd come with such hopes of winning the ten million dollars so she could have her surgery and get pregnant. And with all the money left — think of how she and Ben could provide for their future children. Gina had owned so little in her childhood, she and her parents living in total poverty. She'd dreamed of being a princess and owning a palace. Buying anything she wanted. Today she lived in a nice house with Ben, but it was nothing compared to the houses she sold to rich clients. Why couldn't *she* live in a house like that? If she won this show, she *would*.

Still, none of that mattered more than having a baby. But if Ben found out the truth ...

He couldn't. That's all there was to it. God had shown Gina mercy, forgiving her sin. Her soul had been wiped clean. Since then she'd tried to be the best wife she could possibly be. Her husband did not deserve to be hurt because of her past mistakes. Gina had to work extra hard now to take care of him.

Which meant, at least for the moment, she had to keep lying.

You see that, God, right? You see the predicament I'm in? Besides, You don't seem to be doing anything to stop it.

Gina's conscience throbbed. She ignored it, focusing instead on her next task to fix the situation. She glanced toward the hallway. No one in sight.

She slid forward on the couch, back straightening, and turned a little to face the closest camera. She tried to smile but knew it came out crooked. "Well, not much going on at the moment, huh. No one's talking here in the house. And three people are still gone. Are you watching them somewhere else? I sure hope so. I hope they're keeping you entertained." She lifted a shoulder.

"As for the *clues*"—Gina made quote marks in the air with her fingers—"they're not making much sense. The last one about me going to some restaurant? I don't even remember that. I don't think it happened. And besides, anything *Dream Prize* does know about us contestants should have come from our applications. So either they're making this stuff up, like with my clues—or they had to go snooping into people's private lives to know certain things, like with Tori and Craig. Why would they do that? What gives them the right?"

Gina turned her head to gaze out at the ocean.

"You know what else? This whole concept is messed up. Everyone going around judging everybody else. Like George Fry said—trying to find the worst in each other. That's supposed to be *fun*? Entertaining? You've seen what it's done to people here. No one gets along. Fighting and accusing. Manipulations and lies." Gina's throat tightened. "This isn't good. It's ... demeaning.

Exhausting. There's no love here, only ... I don't know. Pointlessness. I mean, I know we're each trying to win a big prize, and there's a point in that. But being here in this environment, getting *to* that win—it feels ..." Gina spread her hands and focused on the floor. "Shallow. Godless." She shook her head. "And very scary."

Her throat began to burn. Sit here any longer and she'd start crying. Gina had done enough of that.

She took a cleansing breath and focused again on the camera. "Know what I'm going to do? Go for a walk on the beach. That's God's beautiful creation out there. I might as well enjoy it."

Chapter 25

Ten minutes before one. Every second was an eternity.

Shari slumped in a chair, her stomach growling and nerves humming. She'd been stuck in this dank, dim room for nearly twenty-four hours, now with two men—and no way to get out. The world was watching, and nobody even *cared*. No one had come to rescue them, no matter how many times Shari had begged the viewers out there to *do* something. Call the cops, the FBI, rattle somebody's cage until they contacted the Australian police. *Do something*!

Aaron sat across the room, staring stupidly at his notebook. What did he think—answers about everybody's sin would jump out and bite him? Good luck with that. Like it mattered anymore. Lance was hulking around like a big dumb bear, staring at the floor. He'd already eaten most of their food. Next time he went to open the refrigerator door, Shari was going to stop him. She didn't care what she had to do.

These two men—they apparently deserved to be here. They'd both done something terrible. What had Shari done? Blown up her beginning career by going home to care for her sick mother, that's what. For *two years*. Only after her mom died had Shari returned to California. After such sacrifice, who could blame her for what she'd done in the past to try winning a part? Shari had paid her dues.

Aaron's head came up. "Two o'clock in less than an hour. Vote announcement time. Somebody might come through the door."

Lance shrugged. "Who knows. Your own timing doesn't support that theory."

"We have to be ready, in case. One of us needs to guard the door. The minute someone opens it, we stop it from closing."

"Won't get us out," Shari said. "The top door will already be locked."

Aaron stood. "We'll be one step closer. Long range plan. We then guard the top door. Someone comes through at eight o'clock—we're out of here."

Hope spiraled through Shari, then crashed. She eyed the camera lens. "But they'll know what we're doing."

"So? It's entertainment. Everyone will watch to see if we escape."

Shari wasn't so sure. *Dream Prize* wasn't a reality show anymore. It was a horror flick. "Maybe. And maybe they'll send no one else down here, just to stick it to us."

"I'll play guard," Lance said.

"*I* will." Aaron picked up a chair, his notebook tucked under his arm.

"You don't trust me? I'm bigger."

"I'm faster." Aaron set the chair down by the door. "It opens, I'm here."

Shari checked her watch. Almost an hour to wait …

Chapter 26

When Craig entered the great room just before two o'clock, Gina and Tori were already there. Gina fidgeted before the monitor, hitting her notebook with a knuckle. Tori stood at the sliding door, looking out at the ocean. She heard his footsteps and glanced over her shoulder. Met his eyes briefly and turned her back on him.

Hatred spiraled through Craig. The woman thought she was so great. So in control, everyone at her beck and call. She'd treated Nate horribly. Telling him she loved him one minute, then giving him the total cold shoulder the next. The guy had wanted to marry her. She'd so crushed him that he could barely function at work. There were days he didn't show up at all.

Nate deserved so much better than Tori. He didn't deserve anything that had happened to him.

"Hi," Gina mumbled to Craig. She didn't smile.

Craig nodded to her but said nothing. This woman had her own issues. Just ask Aaron.

At precisely two o'clock the monitor began to lighten, and the *Dream Prize* logo appeared. Craig watched the screen.

Come on, come on.

Gina glanced at Tori, who remained by the door, too far away to see what was on the screen. She made no move to come closer. Apparently thought she'd catch some disease if she stood too close to Craig.

Good. She could stay a mile away, for all he cared.

The show's logo faded. Text appeared.

This round's majority of votes go to Craig Emberly.

Craig pumped a fist in the air. "All *right*!"

Gina gasped. "You have *got* to be kidding me." She turned hard eyes on Craig. "*You*? After what you did to Tori?"

Tori lasered Craig with her eyes. "*He* won?"

"Yes." Gina looked like she could spit.

Craig spread his hands. "Such animosity. So sorry to disappoint you ladies."

Tori narrowed her eyes at the nearest camera. "What's wrong with you people? You voted for *him*? After he attacked me? Pushed me to the floor? What kind of people are you?"

"Way to go, Tori." Craig couldn't keep the snide tone from his voice. "Tick off all the viewers, tell them what terrible humans they are. Ought to earn you plenty of votes."

Tori spread her arms, her head shaking back and forth, back and forth. Like she was too revolted for words.

Craig stepped away from the table and gave Tori and Gina a mock bow. "I'll leave you two to your righteous indignation. I take my leave now to pick up my *extra clue*." He emphasized the last two words with a wag of his head.

Swiveling on his heel, Craig headed for his bedroom.

Aaron's Notebook

Monday, 2:15 p.m. Nobody through door.

Aaron's Notebook

Monday, 2:45 p.m. Still nobody.

Aaron's Notebook

Monday, 3:45 p.m. Shari—right. ?? No one will come now?

HOW DO WE GET OUT OF HERE?

Chapter 27

Past four o'clock. No point in waiting any longer for someone to come through the bunker door. Aaron's rear end was numb. He could barely think.

He pushed to his feet and leaned against the cool wall.

Stupid Shari shook her head. "Told you it wouldn't work."

"Shut up."

Aaron closed his eyes. This could not be happening. They couldn't trap three people in this place forever. They had to have a reason, a plan. Whatever the reason was, it couldn't be good enough for what this show was putting them through. This was inhumane. Lock people up and throw away the key? Who did they think they were? How did George Fry and everyone at his network think they could get away with it?

What was this, reality TV turned snuff film?

Heat trickled into Aaron's veins. They could not do this. Could *not!*

The heat kept coming.

His blood got hotter … hotter … until it flowed like lava. What to do with the anger? He couldn't contain it.

He smacked his fist against the thick door. *"Why!"*

"There's a splendid idea, break your hand," Lance threw at him.

The rage kept coming. It would burst Aaron apart. He opened his mouth and yelled. The sound bounced off the walls and back at him. That fueled him more. He yanked up the folding chair. Smashed it against the door. Shock waves shot up his arms, his neck. He didn't care. He smacked the chair again. Again. The door wouldn't budge. Wouldn't *let them out!*

Out-out-out-out-out!

Aaron heaved the chair across the room.

Shari shrieked and leapt up, out of the chair's path. It hit the floor. Skidded. Crashed into the wall.

"Stop iiiit!" She hid her face.

"Calm down, Aaron!" Lance strode toward him.

Aaron shoved out his arms. "Stay back. Stay away from me!"

"Fine, already, self implode if you must. Just leave some chairs for me and Shari to sit on."

Aaron's chest heaved. He staggered to the table. Leaned on it, glaring at the monitor.

"Don't you *dare* touch that thing!" Shari hissed.

Aaron couldn't get enough air. He flicked sweat from his forehead. Pulled in oxygen.

Shari whirled on the camera, her cheeks pink. "Happy now? You *like* watching us all be tortured?"

Lance dragged a chair to the table near Aaron. "Sit down."

Aaron held on to the table until all energy drained away. He slouched into the chair.

Lance eyed him. "Well. Guess we know what deadly sin *you* are.

"Sloth?" Shari cackled like she was losing it.

They were all losing it.

Aaron wiped his mouth with the back of his hand.

The door opened. Craig hurried into the room.

What?

Aaron's brain fought to register.

"Stop!" He shot out of the chair and lunged for the door, Lance and Shari behind him.

Craig blinked. Flung his hands in front of his face and ducked.

The door swung closed.

"Nnnno!" Lance threw himself against it. The door held firm. He grabbed the knob and shook it. Shari pounded the thick wood with her palms.

"What'd you *do* that for?" Aaron launched himself at Craig. Grabbed his shoulders and pushed.

Craig stumbled backward into Shari. They both went down. Shari screamed.

"Hey!" Lance caught Aaron by the arm. Yanked him back.

Shari scrambled away on hands and knees.

Craig shoved to his feet and pivoted toward Aaron. "What's *wrong* with you?"

What was wrong with *him*? "You let the door close!" New anger ricocheted through Aaron. He struggled to free himself. Lance wrapped both arms around his chest and held on.

Craig's eyes bugged. "What are you talking about?"

Aaron still tried to wrench free. Lance shook him. "*Stop!*"

"You're so stupid, Craig!" Shari sprawled on the floor near the table. Tears ran down her face. "Why didn't you *listen*?"

Craig swallowed hard. He tore his eyes from Aaron to Shari. Then looked around the concrete room. He shivered. "What is this place?"

"A bunker." The words fell from Shari like stones. "A trap. They get us in here with a promise they don't keep, then they don't let us out."

Craig's expression flattened. "*What?*"

"The door's locked from the outside, stupid! We were trying to get you to hold it open."

Craig's cheeks paled. "Locked? Right *now?*"

He heaved himself toward the door, but Lance and Aaron were in his way. Craig carved to a stop. "I want out of here."

"You can't leave," Aaron spat. The hold Lance had on his arms infuriated him. He drove his elbow backward into Lance's side. "Let *go!*"

"Ugh." Breath pushed from Lance's mouth. He slid his hands away.

Aaron scurried across the room. He sagged against the wall, panting.

How had he gotten here? This was a nightmare.

"Will somebody please tell me what's going on?" Fear edged Craig's voice. "I just came for a clue. Didn't you? I just want to get it and go. I don't … I can't stay here."

Shari spread her palms on the floor. "Oh, that's funny. Because that's exactly what you're going to do."

"Aaron told you, Craig. You *can't* leave." Lance rubbed his side. "We're locked in here."

"*No.*"

"Yeah. That's the despicable truth."

"I can't—" Craig strode to the door and grasped the knob. Tried to turn it. Wouldn't move. He slapped his other hand on it, wrenching until his fingers whitened. "No!" His face reddened. "*No!*"

He whirled to Lance. "You have to get me out of here!"

"If I could do that, we'd all be long gone."

"But I can't stay! There's no window!" Craig stumbled away from the door, hands flailing. "There has to be — " He staggered along the wall, exploring, slapping the concrete blocks.

"There's nothing, Craig," Lance said, "no hidden tunnel. Maybe with three of us men, we could break through the door. Somehow."

Craig ran to the table. Peered at the dark monitor. He smacked it. "Where's my clue?"

"There *is* no clue!" Shari pushed off the floor and slunk to the farthest corner.

Craig slapped a hand around his throat. "How'd you all get here?"

"Same as you." Lance's tone was flat. "A message sent us."

Craig nodded like a bobble head. "Right. I got a message. After I won at two o'clock. It said to come here. But wait two hours first ..."

Wait two hours?

Aaron pointed at Lance. "They did that on purpose! Because they saw me guarding the door."

"Told you." Shari's mouth pinched. She threw another acidic glance at the camera. "But how'd they know ahead of time you would move, Aaron?"

"They figured we'd give up." Aaron sneered at the lens. "Right, Fry? You didn't tell Shari to wait. Or Lance. Or me. You did this on purpose!" He threw out his arms. "What do you *want* from us?"

"But how do we get out?" Craig shouted. "I have to get *out*!"

How dense was this guy? "You *can't*. Get it? We're *trapped*."

"No." Air stuttered from Craig. "I have to, I *have* to." He stumbled around, his legs like rubber. "I can't stay here. I can't *breathe*."

Understanding hit Aaron. The guy was claustrophobic.

Great. Now they had a lunatic in here.

"Hey, come on, calm yourself." Lance moved toward Craig.

"No!" Craig backed away. "Don't come near me, I need air!" He whipped his head back and forth, then spotted the open door to the bathroom. Hope sprayed across his face. He ran to the room, slapped his palms on both sides of the doorway. Peered inside. His shoulders rose. Then slumped. He spun around and raced to Shari.

"Stay away!" She shrank back.

Craig grabbed her shoulders and shook her. "Help me!"

Shari's head bounced back and forth. She kicked at his shins. "Let me *go.*"

Aaron pulled Craig away. "Stop. Now."

Craig turned on Aaron, hands pummeling. Face contorted. His breath narrowed to a wheeze. "I. Can't. *Breathe.*"

"Get off me, you maniac!" Aaron shoved him away.

Lance strode over. "Craig, calm *down.*" His big hands sliced through the air, trying to pin Craig's. He caught one hand. Aaron grabbed the other.

Craig went limp, his head falling back. He cranked his mouth open. Dragged in oxygen in loud gulps.

"Let him go!" Shari yelled. "Get away from him, you're only making him worse."

The guy could choke for all Aaron cared.

Shari hit Aaron's arm. "Claustrophobics think the walls are closing in, there's no room to breathe. You gotta give him *room.*"

Lance dropped Craig's hand and backed off.

Fine, let the monster loose. Aaron let go.

Craig sank to the floor, gasping.

Keep this up and the guy would lose consciousness. That was the first happy thought for Aaron since he'd gotten here. "Go ahead, Craig, knock yourself out. Literally."

"Hey." Lance locked eyes with Aaron, then Shari. He gestured with his chin toward the bathroom. Headed toward it.

Aaron and Shari hesitated, then followed. Craig stayed where he was, air scraping down his throat.

Disgusting sound.

Lance crowded the two of them in the small room. Banged the door shut. They faced each other, angst-ridden, breathing the same air. But they were out of the camera's sight and hearing.

Lance smacked the lock into place. "Listen." His voice was low. "We must guard the door at all times. Clearly it's their plan to lead all of us down here. And they keep changing how they do it, to catch us off guard. We can't allow that to happen again."

"But what good will it do?" Shari stuck a hand in her hair. Her cheeks were streaked with mascara. "They'll *know* we're guarding it."

"So we break the camera lens," Aaron said.

Lance nodded. "Agreed."

"What?" Shari drew her head back. "No!"

"We have to." Lance wiped sweat from his forehead. "We can't let them see what we're doing anymore."

"But then we'll have *no* contact with the outside!"

Aaron raised his hands. "What good has that done, huh? What can we tell everyone that we haven't already said?"

"But we need them to come get us."

"They already know we're trapped, Shari. If someone hasn't responded by now, they never will."

"Why don't we just cover the lens?"

Lance shook his head. "How? It's flush with the wall, so we can't stuff the hole. Nothing's tall enough to block it off. And we have no way of taping something up there."

Shari stared at him. "But once it's done, it's done. We can't get the camera back."

"We can make one final plea." Lance leaned forward. "Tell viewers to demand that someone rescue us, or we'll die down here. The last thing they'll see is me lifting a chair above my head—and one of its legs coming at the camera." A sick smile twisted his lips. "They want dramatic TV—they shall receive it."

Shari looked from him to Aaron. "You guys are crazy. George Fry said anyone who disables a camera is disqualified."

Oh, no. She was right. Aaron's chin sank.

Lance closed his eyes. "I forgot about that."

"How could you forget *that*?"

"I've been a little distracted."

All of this was so convoluted. Aaron didn't know what to think. "We don't want to be disqualified. But are you sure we're still even *in* the game?"

"Aren't *you*?" Lance asked. "They keep feeding us clues. And you've certainly been studying your notebook."

As if there was anything else to do down here. Irritation knocked through Aaron. He beat it down. "Just—think. If we're still in the game, they have to let us out of here when it's over. That would be tomorrow afternoon. So we wait them out."

Lance frowned. "Then why were you so intent on guarding the door?"

"We still should. If we can get out sooner, great. And viewers want to see us *doing* something. If we're in the game, we're still earning votes."

Shari made a face. "We're sure not being told who's *winning* the votes."

"True." Lance shifted on his feet. "So does that mean we're in or out?"

"We *are* told," Aaron said. "Because the winner walks through the door."

"But what if one of *us* wins? You think they'll tell us? Or leave us waiting for someone else to come through the door?"

"I don't know." Aaron was heating up again. He wanted to hit something. "I think they want us to wonder. So they give us clues but no votes. And they keep the camera running. But remember, just because it's running—doesn't mean they're using the feed. It could be just another trick."

Shari's mouth dropped open. "You mean people may not really be watching us?"

"I don't *know*. They're in control! We're just puppets."

"Well, what would the show tell viewers about us? That we dropped into the ocean?"

An incredible thought hit Aaron. "Maybe they *are* watching, but the show is running statements along the bottom of the screen that tell everyone not to worry, we'll be okay. Because this is all part of the game. That could be why no one's come to rescue us. They're *supposed* to stand by and watch us be tormented."

They fell silent, stunned. Sweat ran down Lance's temple. He smeared it away. Through the door, Aaron could hear Craig still groaning.

"Think about it! Can you *imagine* the show's ratings? They have to be going through the roof right now. Everybody in America is watching this show. *Everybody*. It's gotta be all social media's talking about."

"And Clausto Craig out there?" Shari's voice rose. "They'd just sit back and watch him choke to death?"

"He won't choke to death. He just *thinks* he will. We know they're pushing in air through that ceiling vent. After awhile he'll calm down."

Shari shoved her arms together. "Well, if what you say is true, one thing's for sure. We should all be getting a ton of votes."

Which meant one of them might still win the game. Aaron saw the realization flicker in Lance's and Shari's eyes.

"So." Lance turned his hands palms up. "We just keep doing what we're doing, then? Take turns guarding the door in case anyone else arrives. But otherwise—believe we'll be rescued."

Sudden banging shook the bathroom door.

"Hey!" Craig shouted. "What are you doing in there?"

"Stuff it, Craig!" Aaron kicked the door.

"Let me in!"

"What for? It's an even smaller space in here."

"I need you to— I need ... I have to *get out of here!*"

Great. This again. Craig was going to drive them all insane.

Lance pressed his hefty body against the door. The banging continued. "So we're agreed?"

"What about loony out there?" Shari pointed toward Craig. "Who knows what he's going to do."

Aaron scoffed. "He can't breathe, let alone think straight. I don't even know if he realizes there's a camera here yet."

"That's just my point—when he does, he may be dumb enough to smash it. He might do it so fast none of us can stop him."

"Fine, let him. *He'll* be disqualified."

The banging stopped. Stillness rang in Aaron's ears. What was Craig doing? The bathroom was stuffy, and

Aaron could feel the heat coming off Lance. "We gotta go back out there."

Lance put his hand on the door lock. "Shari, you're the thespian. You want to keep begging viewers to save us early — be my guest."

Shari nodded. "I will."

Lance slid back the lock. "Steady's the word. If Craig falls into hysteria, I'll handle him." He opened the door, letting Shari out first. Aaron followed.

Craig was hovering in front of the table, his mouth open, chest heaving. He pointed a shaky finger at the screen. "Look."

His face suddenly glowed in blue-white light from the monitor.

"Is it the five o'clock clues?" Aaron ran toward the monitor, then stopped. *Where* was his notebook?

There, by the door. Aaron jumped for it, but Lance beat him to it. "That's mine."

Aaron's eyes swept the floor. There, by the refrigerator. He ran to the notebook and snatched it up. Checked the cover. His name was on it.

He hurried to the table and crowded in beside Craig.

"Get outta my space!" Craig shoved him. Fear shone in his eyes.

"Get *over* it, Craig!" Aaron pressed back in.

"Gimme paper! I need a pen!" Craig thrashed around. He grabbed for Lance's notebook.

Lance yanked it away. "No!"

"Gimme yours!" Craig tried to snatch it again.

Lance pushed him. Hard.

Craig stumbled backward. He started to fall, then caught himself.

Aaron saw the *Dream Prize* logo fill the screen.

Focus, man.

He grabbed the pen from his notebook.

Craig jumped toward the monitor. Slapped a hand on Lance's shoulder.

Lance pivoted. "Stay *away* from me!" He swung a fist. Craig jerked away and knocked into Shari.

She kicked Craig's leg. "Go fight somewhere else!"

Chaos all around. Aaron clenched his teeth and stood his ground. *Just focus.*

The logo faded, replaced by text. But it wasn't the list of clues. Aaron read the first two sentences—and froze.

There is only one way out of this room.
You have to EARN it.

Chapter 28

Tori dragged herself into the great room a few minutes before five. Another set of clues to come. Terrific. And her anger at Craig's winning the most votes three hours ago had not subsided. This show was sick. Its viewers were sick. Television had descended into some pretty disgusting territory in the past few years. But nothing like this.

She set her notebook on the table and turned to face the ocean. Should be a soothing sight. But Tori was beginning to hate this house and everything that came with it, including the view. Could she ever hear the surge of ocean waves in the future and not relive these horrible days?

What were the CEO and board of Serros thinking about her right now? Surely they'd heard about the show. The last two clues had painted her as some sort of prowling woman out to break the hearts of younger men. She'd never set out to break anyone's heart. She just ... tended to fall in love easily, that's all. She'd had enough of seeing her own life in ruins thanks to her ex-husband. Ever since she'd pulled out of her black hole of despair she'd wanted the upper hand in relationships. Who could blame her?

What would the next clue say?

Tori squeezed her eyes shut, imagining the smirks of Serros employees when she returned to work.

But if *she* became CEO of the company, it would all be worth it in the end. Somehow she still had to win this thing.

Tori checked the clock on the wall. One minute to go.

Wait. Where was Gina?

A horrible thought crept into Tori's mind. What if she was the only one left in the house?

Footsteps sounded in the hall. Gina entered the room, her flowing pants whispering around her heavy legs. She carried her notebook.

Tori's shoulders relaxed. "Hi." As much as she despised this woman for what she'd done—at least she was still here. "Seen Craig?"

"No. Have you?"

"Not since we were here last."

They looked at each other.

Gina's cheeks paled. "Oh, no. He's not coming, is he."

"I don't know."

"And you wouldn't care. Not after how he came at you."

"Do *you* care that Aaron's not here?"

Gina swallowed. "No. Yes. Because he made number three who's missing."

Tori eyed the doorway. She could hear no one else coming. If Craig was in the house, he'd be here by now. This was not good. Her voice dropped. "Now we just might have number four."

Gina sidled to the table. She opened and closed her mouth, as if struggling with her thoughts. When she spoke, her words were flat, hard. "Do you think they're killing us?"

Something thick and cold trickled into Tori's veins. She forced a laugh. "That's ridiculous."

"Then *what* is happening?"

"I don't know."

Gina dropped her notebook on the table. "You remember that book by Agatha Christie? *Ten Little Indians*?"

A classic mystery Tori had read long ago. She nodded.

"One by one the people in that house disappeared. That's exactly what's happening here."

"Somebody was *killing* those people. This is a television show."

"So *where* is Shari? And Lance? And Aaron, and Craig?"

"I don't know. But I don't think they're dead."

"How do you *know*?" Perspiration glistened on Gina's forehead. "They just disappear and don't come back! And we're supposed to believe they're somewhere else on the island? Doing what? Certainly not playing the game anymore. They're missing the clues. And nobody who's missing has won the most votes after they disappeared, have you noticed that? Why should they—they're not on camera! It's like viewers are being told not to vote for them anymore." Gina's face crumpled. "I don't know what's going on. I just … Tell me you won't leave me, too. You can't!"

"I'm not going anywhere." Gina's anxiety was only ratcheting up Tori's own fear. She tried to push it down.

"Three of them disappeared after winning the most votes." Gina grasped her upper arms. "But Aaron never won, and *he's* gone."

"I won't go anywhere."

"Promise me."

"I won't."

Gina shuddered. "What if someone's coming into the house and taking them?"

"You know that's not true. Lance saw Shari leave."

"He could have been lying."

"But then *he* disappeared. So who's big enough to carry him out of here?"

"Maybe he was drugged."

"Maybe you watch too much TV."

"This *is* TV, Tori, just like you said! Twisted, sadistic TV." Gina pointed toward a camera. "As for Sensation Network, just think about the name. It'll probably end up airing hard core pornography or something. Maybe this will be the *least* bad show on it."

Tori shuddered at the thought. "I vetted the network before even applying for this show, didn't you? I checked out the website and read about their upcoming programming. It all looked fine."

Gina leaned in close, her jaw tightening. "They. *Lied*." She pulled back and waved her hand at a camera. Raised her voice. "It was all lies, wasn't it, George Fry? You got us here through trickery! Now you're telling lies about us through the clues. And people are *disappearing*!"

She pulled her fisted hand to her chest and stared at the floor. Tori felt the chill in her own veins grow colder. What if Gina was right? About everything? Of course she couldn't be. That would be insane.

But what if she was?

Light from the monitor caught Tori's eye. The screen came to life, filling with the *Dream Prize* logo. Their next round of clues was coming.

Please don't be anything bad. Please.

Tori picked up her notebook, slid out its pen—and braced herself.

DREAM PRIZE

Monday 5 p.m.

In late December 2013, five months after *Gina's* dinner at Trancet Restaurant with her former client, the client's wife filed for divorce.

~~~

On January 8, 2014, *Craig's* accountant drove to L.A. to go to a friend's house for dinner.

~~~

On January 8, 2014, after dinner with his mother, *Aaron* left the restaurant in a rage over news she'd told him.

~~~

On May 26, 2012, Kathryn Flex, *Shari's* roommate at the time, was attacked and beaten outside their apartment building.

~~~

On November 15, 2012, the convicted defendant from the trial in which *Lance's* interviewee testified was visited in prison by his brother.

~~~

In late December 2001, *Tori* was admitted to a mental facility for a complete nervous breakdown.

Chapter 29

There is only one way out of this room.
You have to EARN it.

Lance gaped at the monitor. He'd managed to push Craig off—again—and gather his notebook. Craig was now hunched over and leaning against the wall, fighting for air.

Shari gasped at the screen. "What? How?"

"Quiet!" Lance leaned toward the table, trying to take it in. He could barely think in all the commotion. His eyes narrowed as he focused on the menacing words. More must be coming.

"Earn it?" Disbelief tinged Aaron's voice.

"What? What is it?" Craig forced himself up straight and staggered to the table. He peered at the text, jaw hanging open. "I'll do it, I'll do anything!" He pressed both hands against his head, as if his brain might explode any minute. "Tell me *how*!"

They waited. Craig shook the table. *"Tell me!"*

"Stop!" Lance punched his arm.

The two sentences disappeared and new words morphed in.

The camera has been filming, but none of the feed has been seen by viewers. They have been told you are still in the game, and they can still vote for you. They do not know where you are. They do not know you are locked away. No one will come for you. Those left in the house and the boat captain who arrives tomorrow afternoon will be told you have already left the island.

"*Nnno.*" Shari's voice turned into a wail.

How do you earn your way out? The doors will be unlocked ONLY after you confess your secret in front of the camera.

An inconceivable task. A stone dropped through Lance's stomach. He could never do it.

Shari cried harder. Aaron made not a sound. Craig's head kept nodding, nodding, as if he'd accept anything required of him.

As each of you confesses—completely, including dates and places—the others will shut themselves in the bathroom, where they will not hear. After your confession, check the monitor. If you have confessed completely and honestly, your name will appear on the monitor with a check mark. Go immediately to the door, making sure no one else is near. When it unlocks, you have two seconds to open it. The top door will work the same way. NO ONE BUT THE CONFESSOR can go through. If another person forces his or her way through the first door, the top door will NOT unlock—and EVERYONE loses the chance to escape.

Once you are out, return to the house and continue the game. The five o'clock clues you missed will appear on your personal monitor in your bedroom.

Telling other contestants or viewers where you have been disqualifies you from any chance of winning.

You have until midnight to make your decision. After that, the doors will remain locked.

Your confession will be taped but not aired—UNLESS you attempt to rescue another contestant who has refused to confess. In that case, even if the game is over, your confession will air immediately, and if you are the winner, you forfeit your victory.

The heinous words hung on the screen, then slowly faded.

Nobody moved. Lance's pulse thumped in his ears.

Tears ran down Shari's cheeks, smearing what was left of her makeup. "If nobody's seeing the confessions, why do we have to do it?"

Lance's throat ran dry. "So they'll have a weapon to hang over our heads to keep us from rescuing each other."

This show wanted to turn them into *murderers*.

"But what'll they do with the film? Afterwards?"

"I don't know."

Was this about blackmail?

Craig crossed his arms over his chest and backed away from the monitor. "Wait, wait, no. I can't do that, I *can't.*" He stumbled around, muttering at the floor, then jerked toward the camera. His face flushed. "You can't get away with this! Someone will find out, someone will come for us!"

But how long would that take? Lance staggered to a chair and fell into it. He certainly couldn't confess either. But there was so little in the refrigerator. His mind sped up, playing out the interminable days, the fights over food. They would regress into animals. The four of them would kill each other before they starved to death.

Maybe the others would give in and confess. But even then, if Lance did not, he would die alone. Not one of these three people would risk having their confession aired in order to free him.

Would they?

Would *he*, if he were in that position? If he did confess and escape this horrid place—and someone else didn't, whose fault would that be? Besides, whom would he protect—his son or these people?

Lance thrust his head in his hands. Why were they doing this? *Why?* Had he fallen into some nightmare rabbit hole? This could not be *real*.

"George Fry!" Craig shook his fist at the camera. "*Let me out!*" He ran to the door and threw himself against it. Backed up and heaved his body again.

"Craig, stop!" Lance jumped from his chair. The man was going to break his bones—and then imagine the scene he'd cause. Lance grabbed Craig's arms and dragged him away, Craig thrashing to free himself. Both of them tumbled to the floor.

"Craig, calm down!"

"Lemme go, I can't breathe!"

Despair shot through Lance. He pulled his hands off Craig and scuffled to his feet. Fine. He'd had enough fighting for one day. Let the man cripple himself.

Craig squirmed onto his back and gasped for air.

Aaron sagged against the wall, safely out of the way, a sick expression on his face. He watched blankly, as if only half registering the scene.

Lance swiped his forehead. This room was so hot. It had been cool when he first arrived. Were they pumping in warmer air?

He headed for the bathroom on shaky legs. Out in the main room Craig still gasped and Shari cried. The sounds vibrated in Lance's ears.

He turned the sink's cold water handle to rinse his face.

No water came.

Lance stilled. *No.* He shoved the handle for hot.

Nothing.

Lance stared at the sink. They'd turned the *water* off? The comprehension peppered through him like shotgun pellets. He focused on the toilet. They'd have one flush left.

He turned and trotted to the refrigerator, yanked open the door. Counted the water bottles. Five.

Five.

A silent scream rose in Lance's brain. Slowly he closed the door. He locked eyes with Aaron. The man still looked shell-shocked.

"They turned off the water."

"Huh?"

Lance nodded.

Shari stuttered in a breath. "What did you say?"

They both stared at him, then rushed for the bathroom. Lance could see them jerking the sink handles back and forth—until they realized it was useless.

"No." Shari hugged her arms against her body and tottered away from the sink.

Craig pushed himself up from the floor, his face pale. Air dragged in and out of his lungs. "We have no running water?"

Lance shook his head.

Craig reacted like he'd been punched in the stomach. He jerked backward, hands flailing. Stretched his neck out, gulping harder for air. Suddenly he wrenched himself upright and staggered toward the camera. Spread his arms wide. "Okay, okay, I'll do it, I don't even care if they hear! I cheated on my girlfriend. That's it!"

Aaron and Shari sidled from the bathroom, watching him with intensity.

Craig lurched to the monitor. "Come on, *come on,* check my *name.*"

Lance moved beside him to watch.

The screen remained empty.

"Come on! I *told* you! I told you my secret!" Craig pounded the table.

Nothing.

Lance buffed his face with both hands. What Craig had said—it must not be enough. It wasn't *it,* correct? The evil deed, the sinful act the show wanted to extract from him. None of them could lie their way out of this. Because somehow the show creators *knew.* How they knew was beyond Lance's comprehension, but they *did.* The clues had been pointing to the truth all along. Someone, somewhere, was out for their blood. And he and the other three would either tell the truth—or die.

What about Gina and Tori? Why weren't *they* down here?

Lance lost all feeling in his legs. He hung on to the table to stay upright.

"Nothing's happening!" Craig pressed his palms against his head.

Lance barely noticed. The truth was sinking through him like a block of ice. He *couldn't* allow himself to die in here. Leave his son alone, always to wonder what had happened to him? Not even a body to bury. That would be torture for Scott.

There was only one thing Lance could do. Confess and escape this hell hole. Then win the game. With his ten million dollar prize, he'd take Scott and head out of the country—in case the confession ever saw the light of day. They could still live his dream prize of lazing on the beach and playing golf for the rest of their lives. It just wouldn't be in the U.S.

"Where's my *name*?" Spittle flew from Craig's mouth. He grabbed the monitor. "Come *on*!"

Lance pulled his arms away from the screen. "No! Don't break it!"

Craig faced him, chest rising and falling. Lance watched the anger crumble from his face, replaced with despair. "But I *told* them."

"No. You didn't tell them what they want to know, did you. Something far more immoral. Something criminal."

Craig sucked air, in and out, in and out, as if his lungs were rusty billows. His head sank, and he stared at the floor. A single sob escaped him.

"Tell them, Craig." Aaron edged toward him. "Tell them the truth."

Lance met Aaron's eyes, reading his thoughts. Craig was the weakest link, destined to break first. But would this enigmatic game keep its promise? They'd test the system with his confession.

Shari stayed near the bathroom door, hugging herself. Strands of dark hair stuck in her mouth.

Craig straightened. He swallowed hard, fighting for oxygen—then choked. He coughed, his face reddening, then coughed some more. Lance could feel his mounting panic to breathe.

"I *h-have* to g-get out of here!"

"Then *say* it!'

Craig tilted back his head. "Okaaay! You w-want something criminal? I embezzled m-money from my last job. At an ac-counting firm. Five m-million dollars. I used it to—start my f-foundation."

He squeezed his eyes shut, his shoulders slumping. He looked like a broken man. "Th-there."

Wow. Lance gaped at him. So that's where the money came from. All that beneficence for the sick—made possible only through stealing.

Shari's mouth hung open. Aaron hurried over to watch the monitor.

Craig sputtered in a breath and righted himself. He focused on the screen, mouth trembling. "C-come *on*."

His name appeared, followed by a check mark.

"Ahh!" He thrust his hands in the air. "I d-did it!" He swiveled toward Lance and Aaron, waving his arms. "Get away, get b-back so I can leave!"

"No!" Aaron turned toward the door.

"Get *back*!" Craig shoved him.

Aaron stumbled sideways into a chair. It turned over with a crash. He whirled on Craig. "I'm not staying here!"

No, no, no.

Lance stomped toward Aaron. "You have to. If you rush that door, we're all stuck in here. *Forever*."

Aaron glared at him.

Lance planted himself in front of the man, legs apart and arms spread out. Aaron would not get through him. He was a good sixty pounds heavier. "Craig, go."

"But what if—"

"*Go!*"

Craig gasped a breath, then ran for the door.

Aaron tried to jump around Lance. Lance pushed him back. Aaron fell.

Behind Lance, the door clicked open.

"I'm *n-not* rescuing any of you!" Craig shouted.

The door slammed shut.

Lance spun around. Craig was gone.

"He *did* it!" Shari shrieked.

Aaron jumped up and barreled into Lance, knocking him sideways. Lance half fell over his own feet.

"Why didn't you let me *go*?" Aaron's face contorted. "You heard him—he *won't* come back for us!"

Idiot. Lance wanted to knock him out cold. "That should be no surprise to you. Would *you* come back? And you heard the rules. If you'd rushed that door it would be over—for all of us."

"Maybe I'd have made it."

"Through the first door only. Then you'd have gotten us all stuck in here." Lance jabbed Aaron's chest. "I'm not ready to die in here with you!"

Aaron faced Lance, breathing hard.

"You're going next, Aaron."

"*Me*? Why not you?"

"Because I can't keep you away from the door and escape at the same time."

"I'm *not* confessing!"

"You want to die here?"

"Maybe." Defiance marched across Aaron's face. "What's it to you?"

"Nothing. But you're not stopping my chance to get out of here."

Aaron's hard eyes could have cut steel. "What if you did get out? Would you leave this island and let me die?"

"Bet on it."

Aaron's mouth twisted. Then his chest seemed to collapse, as if his energy had just run out. He swung his head away.

Lance threw a look at Shari. She was watching them, wide-eyed. Lance inhaled a slow breath, willing himself to calm. If he didn't free himself from this place soon, he might go as ballistic as Craig.

His gaze fell on a notebook lying on the floor. Lance walked over and picked it up. Aaron's name was on it.

"*Hey —*"

Lance raised a palm. "Just getting it for you." He held out the notebook. Aaron snatched it from his hand.

"Okay." Lance spoke in a level tone. "Shari and I are going to go in the bathroom and shut the door. You can speak quietly, just loud enough for the camera to pick you up. We won't hear."

Aaron didn't move.

"Look, there is no point in delaying this. Nothing is going to change, you know that. We're just puppets, like you said." Lance gestured with his chin toward the camera. "They make the rules."

Emotions rolled over Aaron's face. Fear ... disgust ... disbelief. "*Why* are they doing this?"

Lance sighed. "Wish I knew, Aaron. I wish I knew."

He strode around the table. "Let's go, Shari." Lance picked up two more notebooks from the floor, handing one to her.

She fixed her gaze on Aaron. "*Do* it. Or I'll help Lance beat you to bits."

Lance waited for her to enter the bathroom, then stepped in behind her and closed the door.

Come on, Aaron, come on.

They waited.

Chapter 30

Gina read her clue a second time, heat prickling her veins. *The client's wife filed for divorce.*

She folded over, hugging herself. *Ben.* What was he thinking? Had he believed her claims that the clues were lies? Could he see the truth on her face right now?

She jerked her head up and fought to look defiant. Her cheeks felt wooden.

Gina glanced at Tori. The businesswoman looked just as stricken. And with good reason. A *mental hospital*?

Gina took a deep breath and pulled herself together. She still had to write down the clues. As if from afar, she watched her own fingers move the pen across her notebook.

When the words faded, she and Tori stared at the dark screen.

What were they supposed to do now?

Air rushed from Gina's lungs. She swung her head toward the camera near the great room entrance. "Another lie!" She slapped her notebook down on the table. This time her conscience didn't even prick at her denials. "I didn't even go to that dinner, so what is this clue supposed to mean? *Why* are you saying these things?

And you better not claim *I'm* lying and take away my votes. Because you can't prove *any* of this!"

She turned a hard look on Tori. "Those two clues about you—are they true?"

Tori swallowed. "It's ... they're ..." She pressed her lips. "This is all just garbage. It doesn't mean anything, it doesn't *matter*."

Gina made her way to a couch and sank into it. "So what do we do now?"

Just two of them left. One had to be the winner.

Hope trickled through her veins. Maybe even after all of this ...

But tomorrow afternoon seemed a world away. And they still had two more sets of clues to go. How much worse could they get? Had they really only arrived at this hellish island just yesterday morning?

Plus *four* people were missing. Shari, Lance, then Aaron, and now Craig.

Craig.

Gina stilled. *Craig Emberly.* Suddenly she remembered where she'd heard that last name. Could he possibly be the son of the super rich Emberlys—the family one of her colleagues had sold a house to years ago? The mansion had sold for twenty-five million. An incredible view of the ocean and over twelve thousand square feet. Her realtor friend had marveled that they'd needed all that space when they had only one child. A teenage son.

Gina frowned, recalling the year and doing the math. That son would now be about Craig's age.

Could that be possible? If Craig was that rich, why would he be on this—?

"That clue about Shari." Tori's voice broke into Gina thoughts. "Kathryn Flex was *attacked*? Do you remember reading about that?"

Gina tried to focus on the question. Her mind was still on Craig. "Don't think so. You?"

"No."

"Kind of surprising we didn't."

Tori fiddled with her pen. "Come to think of it, she wasn't famous then. I didn't hear her name until after she starred in *Upside Out.*"

"Oh. Right." Must have been a scary time for Shari. Had she stayed in the same apartment building after that?

A new, horrible thought hit Gina. She thought over Shari's four clues, how they built on each other. Did *Shari* have something to do with that attack?

Gina frowned. No way. That would take a heart of pure evil. Shari was stuck on herself for sure. But she wasn't *that.*

"I think it's time we looked for the others," Tori said.

Gina blinked. "What? Why? You didn't seem concerned about them a minute ago."

"I know. But ... what do we have to lose? If they really are stuck somewhere and need our help ..."

"We have votes to lose if we go through the fence gate."

"So we both go. We both lose votes—we're even." Tori glanced toward the ocean. "But if we do it, we'd better leave soon. We don't want to be caught out there after dark."

Gina focused on the fabric of the couch cushion until it blurred. Tori was right. Besides, Gina didn't think she could spend another sleepless night—now wondering where *four* people had gone. "Okay."

Tori nodded. "I'll change into some walking shoes. And we should check the bedrooms one more time, make sure no one's there."

Another sickening thought ricocheted through Gina's brain. "How do we really know they're not in their rooms?" She pushed to her feet. "Their curtains are all closed, and the doors are locked. What if they *are* in there?"

"Then they'd answer the knock."

"Not if they couldn't. Not if they're *dead*."

Tori gave her a look. "Are you back to that again? Shari was seen *leaving*, remember?"

Gina pressed a hand to her chest. That churning fear deep in her gut just wouldn't go away. Even so, she was aware of the cameras, the viewers. She was closer than ever to winning. "Like I said before, I don't know what's happening. But you've got people missing and clues about us that aren't true. This game is just playing with us, playing with our heads. It hasn't been right from the beginning." Fresh indignation kicked through her. She faced a camera, voice rising. "And how do you expect us to figure out what "sin" somebody else represents, anyway, George Fry? Nobody represents just one sin. We're *all* sinners before God—that's what the Bible says. At one time or another everybody on earth—including you—has probably committed *all* the Seven Deadly Sins. Who are *you* to decide what we are?"

Heat flushed across Gina's cheeks. She gripped her arms, working to calm herself, but the emotions kept swirling with nowhere to go. She needed to *do* something. Keep busy. She turned to Tori. "Let's do it. Find the others."

Gina's conscience wouldn't let her *not* do that. Besides, even if all four came back safe and sound, it would be too late for any of them to win the game. They'd missed clues. And votes.

"I'll go change my shoes, too." She headed for the hallway. "Meet you at the back door in a few minutes."

Tori followed her out of the room.

Of course there was something Gina planned to do first when she got to her bedroom. She'd march straight to her personal camera and turn it on. Before she went looking for the missing contestants she needed to beg viewers for every vote they could cast. After all, she still had to beat Tori.

As Gina neared the bottom of the stairs, Tori close behind, the back door opened—and Craig stumbled inside.

Chapter 31

Shari waited in the tiny bathroom with Lance for what seemed like forever. Again and again she checked her watch. Not a sound came from outside the door. What was Aaron doing? She wouldn't put it past him to just sit there, taunting them in his silence.

What if he didn't confess? What if he kept trying to rush the door? She really could be stuck in here forever. She could *die* here. Seemed crazy to believe. But Shari had lost all faith that George Fry or anybody else at Sensation Network cared a thing about her and the other contestants. This was the entertainment world at its worst. It was all about the money—who cared what happened to the people involved.

Shari broke out in sweat. Lance was already perspiring heavily. It ran down both his temples as he leaned against the door, eyes closed and forehead creased. The man looked like he was barely holding on.

Five minutes passed. No sound.

Amazing—that she'd come to this. Wanting so badly to confess on camera. But it wouldn't matter in the end. All she'd have to do, if the confession ever surfaced, was say she'd lied to save herself. She'd been trapped underground and forced to admit to something terrible. So she'd made up the worst thing she could think of. Who wouldn't understand *that*?

"Do you think he's gone?" Shari whispered.

Lance opened his eyes and looked at his own watch. "Let's give him another five. We don't want to spook him, if he's still thinking it over."

"And if he doesn't do it?"

"We'll *make* him."

"Yeah, right. How exactly are we supposed to do that?"

Lance's eyes narrowed. "Compose yourself just this once, Shari. Give him time."

Shari shoved her arms together. Men thought they knew so much.

They waited. Breathing. Sweating.

Six minutes.

Seven.

Shari's lungs tightened, then her throat. Enough of this. She was starting to feel all Craig-like. "It's been long enough. Open the door."

Lance didn't move.

"Open it!" Shari punched his arm.

Lance grabbed her wrist and held on tight.

"Ow, let go of me!"

He sank his fingers in deeper. "I will not let you ruin this."

She tried to wrench free. "You're acting stupid, he's probably gone. Let *go*."

Lance glared at her, then pushed her away.

She clutched her wrist against her chest, rubbing. Disgusting man. "I'll bet I know your secret—you beat up your wife. Or daughter. Or both."

Darkness twisted his face. "I don't have a daughter or wife. And you have *no* idea what you're talking about."

"Open the door, Lance. I'm not staying in here with you another minute."

He threw her a disdainful look, then moved away from the door. Nudging it open, he peered outside.

Shari's heart ground into a forceful beat. *Please, Aaron, please.* She craned her neck to see around Lance. "Is he there?"

Lance opened the door farther, then stepped out into the bunker. Shari crowded behind, head swiveling.

No Aaron.

No Aaron!

Air gushed from Shari's mouth. She bent over, weak with relief. They were closer to freedom. One step closer to getting *out* —

What if George Fry changed the rules again? Said she had to stay?

No, no, no. Panic jerked Shari up straight. "I'm going next. Right now. I have to go *right now!*"

No way was she being left here alone. Fry would let her *starve* to death.

She pushed Lance. "Go! Get back in there! I'll be fast."

Lance eyed her—then nodded. He turned and disappeared into the bathroom. The door clicked shut.

Please let me go after this, please, please. Half of Shari still didn't believe she was doing this.

She took a deep breath and faced the camera. She had to look a total mess. And for once in her life, she didn't care.

"Here's my confession." Shari kept her voice low. ""In May of 2012 I learned my mom had cancer and needed me. Even though it would hurt my career, I left California the very next day to go back home and nurse her ..."

Chapter 32

Craig took in the shocked faces of Gina and Tori. Both women were frozen on the stairs, staring at him as if he were a ghost.

He felt like one.

And he had to look a sight. Sweaty, wild-eyed, his clothes dirty. Swaying on his feet. Had he really been locked in that room less than two hours? It felt like a lifetime.

Gina blinked. "*Where* have you been?"

Questions. Here they came. Craig had no energy to deal with them. "Out."

"Out where?"

"What's it matter to you?"

"You missed the five o'clock clues—it must be somewhere important."

Craig shrugged.

Tori moved down a stair, beside Gina. "Were the others with you?"

"I can't tell you anything. Let's just leave it at that."

"Leave it at that?" Gina's mouth tightened. "Can you at least tell us if the others are okay? We were just going to go look for them."

"I can't tell you anything." Craig headed for the bedroom hallway, his legs still weak. "Don't waste your votes looking for anyone."

"What's *that* supposed to mean?" Gina called after him. "Are they *dead*?"

He raised his arms.

"Craig, come on!"

He reached his door. Slid his key in the lock and escaped inside.

Finally.

Craig shut the door, leaned against it, and *breathed*. Even though his curtains and sliding door were closed, and the air was stuffy, it was a hundred times better than the bunker.

For a long moment he couldn't move. Then slowly rational thought back to return. So much to do now, so very much to do. He had to calm himself. Get back in the game.

Craig's gaze fell on his notebook, lying on the desk where he'd left it. The five o'clock clues were on his monitor, just as they'd been promised. He moved closer and studied them, still trying to bring his mind around. Finally he sat down and wrote them in his notebook.

By the time he was done with that task, his pulse had fallen to near normal.

In the bathroom Craig guzzled water, then took a long shower. Under the soothing spray, he felt steadiness return to his nerves. He'd done it. Actually done what he'd had to do. Now he was safe in his room. It would do no good to look back, relive those terrorizing moments. Now he had to go forward.

Game on.

Craig rubbed shampoo into his short hair.

How long would it take for the other three to crack? Would they push their decisions right up to the midnight deadline? He pictured them still in that room, agonizing over whether to confess their terrible truths—or die.

Craig closed his eyes and smiled as the water ran over his head and face.

By the time he was dressed again, the bunker almost seemed like a bad dream. Craig was starved. He locked his room and headed upstairs to the kitchen.

Chapter 33

Light. Fresh air. *Sun.*

The warmth on Aaron's face had never felt so good. He shuffled away from the shed, gripping his notebook. Laughing. Crying. Limp with relief, despite what he'd been forced to do. He was free. *Free.*

He fell to the ground and sat, elbows on his knees. Long, deep breaths. *Feeling* the day.

Aaron stayed there until he could breathe right again. Until the trembling went away. Then he stayed longer.

At the house he'd have to face people.

Footsteps pounded behind him. Aaron jerked around. Shari was running up the path as if chased by a monster. Her face was white, her makeup streaked black. Without a word she veered around him and kept going.

Aaron heard the backyard gate swing open. Crash shut.

Lance would come soon. Aaron did not want to face *him* again. But he sat another minute before pushing to his feet. He needed to get to his room. Get his head on straight. Read the five o'clock clues. Shower. Eat.

Aaron started for the house. As he walked through the gate he saw movement on the upper deck.

Tori. Staring down at him.

"Aaron! Where have you been? Did I just see Shari run in?"

Questions, questions. No time for them. Aaron kept walking.

"Hey, talk to me!"

He entered the house. Headed for his bedroom and locked the door. The room was stuffy. He'd had enough of that. He opened the sliding door and curtains to light, moving air.

If someone peeked in his room, he would deal with it.

Aaron checked his monitor. The clues were there.

Sudden grim reality avalanched over his head.

Even if his confession was never revealed, would the clues alone lead viewers to the truth?

He read his own clue first.

On January 8, 2014, after dinner with his mother, Aaron left the restaurant in a rage over news she'd told him.

No.

Aaron gripped the back of the chair. They *were* doing it! Leading right up to the events of that night. Why did they even *need* his confession?

He read Gina's clue.

In late December 2013, five months after Gina's dinner at Trancet Restaurant with her former client, the client's wife filed for divorce.

Aaron's lip curled. *Tell me something I* don't *know.*

He sat down. Shut his eyes. The facts were building up quickly. And two more clues were still to come.

Why were they doing this?

Why had he confessed? He should have stayed strong in that bunker, thought of some other way to escape. If Lisa learned what he'd done that night, she'd never love him.

Dark, cold dread seeped through Aaron. He could not let it stay. He had to *think*.

He opened his notebook and wrote down the clues.

His stomach growled. He ignored it.

Aaron studied the clues. The dates for his and Craig's new clues were the same.

Aaron's jaw slowly unhinged.

No. Couldn't be.

Didn't fit.

He went back in his notebook and studied the old clues. Added facts about each person together. What did he know for sure? What did he *not* know?

He really needed to win the next round of most votes so he could earn an extra clue. But he'd been off camera for so long. Nobody would be voting for him right now.

Would they even really *give* an extra clue to the winner? Until now that promise had been only a trick. He certainly wouldn't fall for that again.

Aaron turned and gazed at the yacht picture above his bed.

Lisa.

She'd said he was too impatient. Not kind enough. She didn't know him. He *loved* her. He would show her.

This is all for you, Lisa.

Aaron turned back to his notebook and picked up his pen.

Aaron's Notebook

Monday, 6:30 p.m.

Gina/me: mother-files divorce 12/13. 1/8/14 dinner-tells me-about father's affair.

Gina: Lust ?(affair)

Craig: accountant in L.A.—dinner w/ friends 1/8/14. (Same date.) Friends—who? Find out.

Craig: Greed? (embezzled money)

Craig's clues re: accountant must lead to his secret of embezzlement. How? Acct.'s friends at dinner—knew? Told him?

Shari: pic in bedroom w/ Kathryn Flex. Brochure on Shari's desk—Sundowner Apts.—where K. attacked. Clue #3—K. loses role in Last Bend. Due to attack?

Shari: Pride (SO in love with herself)

Lance: convicted defendant from trial—who?
Defendant's brother visited him in jail. Who is brother?
Importance? <u>Find out.</u>

Lance: ?? Gluttony? (But how connected to trial?)

Tori: Nervous breakdown 2001. So...?

Tori: ?? Envy?

Me: sin-N/A

Chapter 34

At five minutes before eight, Gina entered the great room for the most votes announcement—and saw all five other contestants gathered.

Whoa.

No one was talking, and a new level of tension hung in the air. Gina had already seen a worn and jumpy Lance in the kitchen, making dinner. She'd peppered him with questions as to where he'd been. He was no more help than Craig. Now Gina marched up to Shari, looked her in the eye and demanded to know where she'd gone.

No answer. None. Shari's makeup and hair were perfect, as if she'd just stepped from a salon. *Bet she didn't come back looking like that.*

As for Aaron, Gina wouldn't go anywhere near the man.

She stood away from the group huddled around the monitor and spread her arms. "Well, thanks a lot, all four of you. Tori and I were in a panic, thinking you were hurt or something. Maybe dead. You could at least tell us what you were doing."

Gina scanned their faces. Lance and Craig just shrugged, and Shari ignored her. Aaron glared.

"*Why* did you leave? Who told you to go?"

It must have been a message on their bedroom monitors. Right? How else would they know to leave the house?

Tori shook her head. "Don't bother, Gina, I've already tried. You'll get nothing."

"I can see that. How about the clues yesterday? Did you miss them, or get them somewhere else?"

No response.

"Come *on*, people, you can tell me that."

"We don't have to tell you anything," Lance declared.

Great. Just great.

Gina focused on Craig. She had a few more things to demand from him when she could get him alone. But right now she was sick of all of them. Sick, sick, *sick*.

She turned her back and gazed at the ocean.

Gina had to admit there was one good thing about the four of them being gone for so long. They'd been off camera. Right? If so the most votes winner would likely be either her or Tori. Finally Gina had a decent chance of winning a round, especially with all the time she'd spent talking to viewers in her bedroom.

Surely by now viewers (Ben!) believed the clues about her were false.

Gina had told viewers even more. She'd plunged in and described the surgery she wanted, the baby she and Ben so longed for. At this point, she *had* to. And who wouldn't empathize with her now? Meanwhile, what did Tori have to talk to viewers about? Multiple relationships with younger men. And a mental breakdown. *That* was sure to impress people.

Gina hugged her notebook. Fear still gnawed at her, and she hated that. She should be confident. But what if she really did win the most votes this time? Every person who'd won had *disappeared*. And they'd come back looking terrible.

Was that just coincidence? Aaron had never won, and he still went … wherever.

He should have stayed gone.

Gina looked at the clock. Almost time. She edged close enough to the table to read the monitor—and held her breath.

The *Dream Prize* logo appeared.

This round's majority of votes go to Gina Corrales.

Tori made a disgusted sound in her throat.

Gina's jaw dropped. *Really?*

She'd done it!

She looked at Lance, then Shari. Neither would meet her eyes. Aaron looked downright smug. Craig shook his head and started for the door.

They knew something bad would happen to her. Didn't they.

Keep calm, girl. You can do this.

Gina faced the camera near the room's entrance. "Thank you!" She managed a big smile. "Thank you so much."

She hurried out of the room, wanting to catch Craig before she went downstairs.

"Craig, wait!"

He ignored her, heading for the kitchen. She followed but kept her distance. This man had attacked Tori.

Craig opened the refrigerator door. "Hadn't you better get to your room for the extra clue, Miss Winner?"

Wasn't he back to being Mr. Cool? Gina stopped at the center island. "I know who you are."

He rummaged in the deli drawer and pulled out a package of cheese. Shut the fridge door. "What's that supposed to mean?"

"Your parents—the Emberlys. They're rich. Multi, multi millionaires."

Craig threw her a dismissive glance. "You've got me mixed up with someone."

"No, I don't. I know because a friend of mine sold your parents a house. You were a teenager."

"Teenager? That would have been a long time ago."

"It was."

Craig opened the cheese and peeled off three slices. Stuffed one in his mouth.

"And the teenager's name was Craig." Gina wasn't sure that was true, but maybe it would flush him out.

Craig chewed and swallowed. "Okay. So what do you want from me?"

Wow, it really *was* him.

Gina planted a fist on her hip. "Why are you in this game? You don't need ten million dollars."

"The prize doesn't have to be money, you know that."

"But you can buy whatever you *want*. And growing up in your powerful family in Southern California, you must have all sorts of famous friends."

"What do my friends have to do with anything?"

"It's just that … The rest of us are normal people. You're not. So *why* are you here?"

"Just because my parents are rich, that doesn't mean *I* am. They're all about making me earn my own way."

Gina stopped short. Was that true? "I think you're lying. I'll bet you're set with some huge trust fund."

Craig brought another slice of cheese to his mouth, then lowered it again. "Believe what you want. Maybe ten million doesn't sound like much to you, but it's a lot for my foundation. Yes, I have a lot of wealthy friends who have donated funds. But if I win, every cent of that prize money is going to help people with M.S., like my niece. Even if I don't win, I'm getting extra publicity for the Craig Emberly Foundation, which will lead to more donations. And—in case you're wondering—no, none of the foundation money goes in my pocket. Not one cent. I don't even get paid a salary. I have at least enough to live on." Craig gestured toward the camera behind Gina. "There are thousands of people out there who suffer from M.S. I know they're grateful that their plight is being heard on such a highly watched show. *That's* why I'm here." The piece of cheese went into Craig's mouth. "So—what do you intend to do with *your* dream prize?"

Gina felt her cheeks flush. Her reason for wanting the money had seemed so worthy. But it was all to make her own life better.

Leave it to Craig to make her feel like she should apologize for dreaming of having a baby.

Gina turned and strode out of the kitchen, chin high.

Arguing voices drifted from the great room as she walked toward the stairs. Sounded like Lance and Aaron. Shari and Tori were coming out of the room, bad vibes shimmering between them.

This whole house was a cesspool of hatred.

Gina sped up and beat the women to the stairs. She hurried down them, mind spinning as to what special information she would ask for now that she'd gotten her answer about Craig. *If* she got an answer at all. If some weird message telling her to go somewhere came up—forget it. No way was she leaving the house all by herself. Not after seeing how cool man Craig looked when he'd returned.

In her bedroom Gina locked the door and tossed her notebook on the desk. It was so hot. She opened her sliding door and curtains. With a huff, she sat down on her bed and frowned at the floor, thinking. After a few minutes she got up and fetched her notebook, poring over the last set of clues. She'd made numerous notes about the ones for Lance. They seemed so carefully worded and odd—more about some person he once interviewed than about Lance himself.

Unless the defendant in that trial *was* Lance.

Gina gazed at the ocean, barely registering the view as she thought that over.

She sat down at her desk and switched on the camera. The green light glowed.

"Hi. I want to know the name of the convicted defendant in that trial mentioned in Lance's clues."

She waited, eyes fixed on the monitor.

Please, please.

After a forever minute, text appeared on the screen.

The defendant's name is Douglas West.

Gina let out a breath. An answer! Just a plain answer. But it wasn't "Lance."

She wrote the name down in her notebook, then spoke it aloud for the viewers.

"Talk to you later." Gina shut off the camera.

A knock sounded on her door. Gina jumped. "Who is it?"

"Tori. I just wanted to see if you're okay."

Of course. Not that the woman really cared if Gina disappeared like the others. "I'm fine."

"You're not going anywhere?"

Matter of fact, Gina didn't plan to even move from her bedroom until morning. "Not a chance."

"Good." A pause. "Did you get an answer to your question?"

Gina flicked a look at the ceiling. "Tori. I'm fine. Okay?"

Nosy woman.

"Okay."

Gina eyed the door, half expecting another question to filter through it. But—silence.

She turned back to her notebook. Where was she?

Douglas West.

Gina frowned. Now what? The defendant wasn't Lance, so what difference did this even mean?

She should have asked a different question.

Then again, maybe none of it mattered. In the end all she had to do was guess which of the Seven Deadly Sins Lance represented.

The guy ate a lot. He had to be Gluttony.

Shari's Notebook

Monday night

Can't wait to get out of here! These people are horrible, and the game is unfair and just ridiculous. (Understatement!) Wonder if I can sue? Sure gonna try. Would keep me in the headlines. <u>Note—call lawyer soon as I get home.</u>

SO tired. No sleep last night. To bed early.

Viewers love me. I'm gonna win!!!

Maybe I won't sue. Not if I win.

<u>*Recap of clues so far:*</u>

Gina—maybe had affair with some client? Who'd be attracted to <u>her?</u> And—who cares? People have affairs all the time. ??

Craig—M.S. foundation. Weird stuff about accountant. So??

Aaron—BO-RING. Went to computer convention, went to dinner with his mother. Get a life.

Lance—interviewed guy who testified in trial. So? How related to Lance?

Tori—a COUGAR!! Hah! Plus—had a breakdown years ago. So do half the people in Hollywood. Who cares?

All these clues—dumb. Make no sense. But they must link to tell a story. Like mine ...

<u>Sins:</u>

Gina— Gluttony (fat)

Craig—?

Aaron—Wrath? (mad a lot). Pride? (acts like he's so great)

Lance—?

Tori—Lust (cougar!)

Me—none

DREAM PRIZE

Day Three

Tuesday, March 8

Chapter 35

Tuesday morning Tori woke before dawn, her mind in high gear. The last day—and on a heightened schedule. Clues at nine and two, with a vote winner announcement at noon. Everyone's answer had to be locked in by three o'clock.

So much to accomplish in the next few hours.

If the people who'd disappeared hadn't received clues while they were gone, they would be very interested in hearing what they'd missed. Tori could negotiate a careful exchange of information.

Her insides bubbled. What would the last two clues about *her* say?

What if she *didn't* win?

She pushed the thoughts aside. This was crunch time. She knew how to handle pressure.

Tori stared at the ceiling.

Why were Gina's and Aaron's clues linked, as well as hers and Craig's? Tori should know that by now. It wasn't coincidence. No way.

Maybe contestants whose lives overlapped had been chosen just to make the show more interesting. Viewers could watch them become aware. A story with twists. Not to mention fodder to make the six of them fight each other.

That in itself was reason enough.

Tori hauled herself from bed and into the shower, then took extra care with her makeup and hair. She put on pale pink shorts and a multi-colored short sleeve silk top. Slipped into designer sandals of pink and white. She studied herself in the mirror and smiled. Almost twenty years older than Shallow Shari, and Tori looked every bit as good. Maybe better. And it was much harder keeping a figure at her age.

Tori slipped out of her room to make coffee. She'd brew a big pot, enough for others. How kind of her. Something the viewers would notice.

She needed their votes.

And apparently winning the most votes was no longer dangerous.

Only she and Aaron had not yet been a vote winner. Not that Aaron deserved *any* votes. But then neither had Craig, after he'd attacked her, yet he'd been that very session's winner.

So much for the viewers' taste.

Passing the back door, Tori peered outside. Another beautiful day was dawning. Not that she could enjoy it.

She veered toward the stairs.

All the same, Tori would appeal to the viewers' softer sides—as much as possible. If somebody came at her, she'd fight back. But she feared she was already viewed as a tough, brassy female. The old stereotype of a woman in business.

Tori sighed.

Those viewers who weren't judging her for being too strong might judge her for being "too weak," thanks to the last clue about her mental breakdown.

Sometimes you can't win for losing.

Tori reached the top of the stairs and turned right. The kitchen was empty. Fine with her. The clock on the stove read six-fifteen.

She made the coffee, poured herself a large mug, added cream and headed back down the stairs. In her bedroom she opened her sliding door and pulled back the curtains just enough to let some breeze in. She gazed again at the waking day. If only she could sit out on the deck and enjoy her coffee. Take a walk on the beach.

With another sigh, Tori sat at her desk and opened her notebook. For a few minutes she studied the clues and all her notes on interactions with the other contestants. When she was ready she took a deep breath and turned on her camera.

"Good morning." She smiled. "It's the last day here, with the big reveal at four o'clock. Things could get pretty crazy. I can only imagine how you all must be trying to piece the clues together and come up with something that makes sense. I'm doing the same thing. So, just as I do at work when faced with a difficult task, I've tried to break everything down, study the facts from different angles. Here's what I've come up with so far. I'm *not* locking these in as my final statements, understand. This is just where I am so far."

Tori paused for a drink of coffee. The action should make her look calm, relaxed.

"Going down in the order of clues, first you have Gina. After seeing the first three clues about her, it seemed clear to me that she had an affair with Aaron's father. Of course she denied this and continues to do so, which is understandable. Not a great thing to have announced on national television. But yesterday morning in the great room I slipped a note to her — remember that? My note accused of her having the affair. And Gina nodded, admitting it was true." Tori's eyebrows rose. "What's more, we now know that affair broke up the marriage of Aaron's parents."

Tori folded her hands and rested them on the desk. "As for which of the Seven Deadly Sins Gina represents, it would be easy to say it's Lust, since she had an affair. In fact for a time I was sure she's Lust. But I'm rethinking that. Remember Aaron. How long did it take him to finagle his way into Shari's bedroom? Only a few hours. *That* speaks more of intentional sexual pursuit, if you ask me. An affair involves lust, sure. But I think at the heart of all affairs is just plain selfishness. Somebody wants what they want *when* they want it. And it doesn't matter who gets hurt —"

Tori broke off abruptly. Her gaze fell to the desk. This one-sided conversation was edging a little too close to home.

She looked up, managing a tight smile. "Actually, maybe all sin is like that. I'm no Bible reader or church goer, but it seems to me sins are about *today* — gratification now. The short term view. Long term … well. Once the mistakes are made, things don't always work out so great."

Tori reached for the coffee mug. The warm drink felt good going down her clenched throat.

"So I'm not sure what Gina is. Maybe Pride." Tori twisted her mouth. "She has a way of acting like she's … above all this somehow."

Tori focused on her notebook.

"Next is Craig. At first he seemed like such a nice guy." She scoffed. "He's pure judgment. And quick to anger. Just look what he did to me. I think he's Wrath.

This does not come from his clues. It comes from watching the way he acts. That's half the game anyway. Words can only say so much about a person.

"Third is Aaron. As I already noted, I think *he's* Lust." Tori paused.

"Fourth on the list is Shari. I know she's talked a lot to you viewers. And a lot of you have voted for her. But she never seems satisfied. I'll bet you've noticed that. As if she's always thinking, 'Come on, give me more and more votes.' She just might be Greed. That's one sin that can be more subtle then, say, Lust. Greed can be largely in the mind. It's about not being satisfied with what you have."

Something twinged inside Tori, and she reached for her mug to cover her uneasiness. *She* wasn't satisfied with what she had, either.

She took a long drink of coffee, that thought pulsing in her head.

But so what? When it came right down to it, who *was* satisfied?

Tori set down the cup.

"Number five—Lance. He's a real puzzle. Seems to keep a lot inside and was clearly rocked by the two clues I saw him receive—the ones on Sunday. I need to find out more about Lance."

Tori spread her hands. "Which brings us to me. I'm pretty open. What you see is what you get. I try to read people and figure out the best ways to approach them. Communicate with them. That's just something an executive needs to do. So ..." Tori cocked her head. "Do I represent one of the Seven Deadly Sins? I honestly don't think so." She smiled. "But I'll let you decide."

She took a final drink from her mug.

"Well, my coffee's all gone. Time to get some more. See you again upstairs."

Tori stood, and with a final nod, turned off the camera.

She stepped back, proud of herself. Now *that* ought to win some votes.

Chapter 36

Lance tossed and turned Monday night, haunted by the last two clues about himself. First, the defendant's conviction in the trial. Second, the man being visited by his brother in jail. Imagine having to see family only through a glass window in prison.

But enough about that man. What about Lance *himself*? These slowly revealed facts were tightening the noose around his neck, even if his confession was never released.

Lance flopped onto his back, staring at the dark ceiling. His thoughts segued to clues about the other contestants.

Who'd have guessed about Gina? She'd had an affair with *Aaron's father*? If the man was anything like his son, he and Gina would make quite the unlikely pair. Unless the clues referenced two different clients. Even so, Gina had at least been the realtor for Aaron's parents. That connection could not be coincidence. In addition, five out of six contestants were from California. And even Aaron's clues were about a trip he took to L.A.

What did all this mean?

Lance twisted onto his side. The pillow felt uncomfortable. He punched it to better support his neck.

What happened to Gina after she won the most votes? Lance hadn't seen her the rest of the evening. Had she gone to the bunker? What criminal act had she committed that Fry would force her to confess? Something involving the mentioned client, most likely. Aaron's father again? How long had it taken Gina to crack in the bunker? Two minutes?

When morning finally dawned Lance rolled out of bed with sore muscles and zinging nerves. This was the climactic day. By tonight he'd be back in the mainland hotel. Tomorrow he'd be on a plane to Sacramento.

Home seemed so far away.

Lance stepped into the shower and let warm water flow over his throbbing head.

Why had George Fry gone to such great lengths to extract four confessions when he already seemed to know everyone's secrets? Would he break his promise and release the videos?

What did Lance's own confession matter? That crime was solved, the defendant in jail. The prosecutor wouldn't want to reopen that case. He'd *won*.

Lance picked up the soap.

As he lathered his body he worked to convince himself the confessions would never be aired. Fry had gotten what he wanted—to petrify the four of them. The man was a sadist. He'd probably laughed his head off, witnessing their agony.

But what if Fry *did* break his promise?

Not a gamble Lance could take. As soon as he got home, he and Scott would have to leave the country. But their windfall of money was long gone, and they had little saved.

Lance *had* to win today.

He stepped out of the shower and dried off. Pulled on a clean pair of baggy shorts and a red T-shirt.

His nerves shimmied.

He found himself staring at the courtroom photo above his desk, imagining some *Dream Prize* minion printing that picture and framing it. How planned all this had been.

Scott.

A vise gripped Lance's chest. Once again he had to save his son. He had to *win*. But the hours in the bunker had cost him. He was nowhere ready to solve this game.

Lance pressed a fist against his mouth. He had to gather information fast. *Now.* At whatever cost. He'd beat it out of people if he had to.

Time was ticking.

Jaw clenched, Lance snatched up his notebook and left the room.

As he passed the door next to his, it opened. Shari stepped through it.

Lance reacted almost before his brain could register. He jumped into the threshold, knocking Shari backward. Strode into her room and slammed the door. He locked it.

Shari careened into her desk, then flailed upright. Her face flushed crimson. "Get *out* of here!"

Lance stood with legs apart, absorbing the data of the room. Above the desk hung a picture of Shari and her ex roommate, actress Kathryn Flex.

"Get *out*!" Shari pummeled Lance's chest with both fists.

With no effort he pinned her arms, his eyes sweeping over the other two photos. A hospital room. A movie theater sign.

Hospital.

Shari struggled, cursing. She jerked up a knee. Lance pivoted, and it caught him in the thigh.

"You stupid—" He shoved her to the floor.

She screamed.

Somebody banged on the door. "Shari!" Tori's voice.

"*Help-me-Lance-is-in-here!*" Shari scrambled away from him.

"Lance!" More pounding. "Open the door!"

He stood over Shari, mouth twisting. That hospital picture. The sob story Shari had told him in the bunker about leaving California to nurse her mother. He understood now.

Shari was even worse than he'd imagined.

"I know what you did to your mother."

Shari stilled, one hand against her mouth. Her face contorted. "I didn't do anything but help her!"

"You really believe that, don't you. She was dying anyway, you rationalized it all in your mind."

"I—"

"Who's in there?" Aaron's muffled voice came from the hallway.

"It's Lance!" Tori said. "He's hurting Shari."

"Aaron, help me!" Shari screamed.

The man's hard laugh filtered through the door.

"*Do* something, Aaron!" Tori's voice.

"Not my problem." His words faded down the hall.

Shari widened her eyes.

Lance sneered at her. "See? Nobody cares about you. Just like you didn't care about your *mother.*" He moved away from her, disgusted at their mere proximity. How could she hurt a helpless member of her own *family?*

His notebook lay on the floor. He snatched it up.

"Open the door, Lance!" Tori banged again.

He flung it wide. Tori's fist froze midair.

"She's all yours." Lance pushed past Tori into the hall.

Tori started into the room. "Shari, are you—"

"Get out! Leave me alone!"

Tori backed off. The door slammed.

Lance headed for the stairs.

"What did you *do* to her?" Tori flung the words at his back.

He waved a hand and kept walking.

Nothing like what she did.

Lance thudded up the steps, churning with disdain and wrenching satisfaction.

He veered into the kitchen. Aaron stood at the refrigerator, right where *he* needed to be.

"Get out of my way." Lance threw his notebook on the center island.

Aaron ignored him, taking his sweet time pulling out eggs and a package of bacon.

"You do *not* want to mess with me today, Aaron."

"Yeah?" He put the items on the counter. Opened a cabinet below the cooktop and brought out a pan.

"I'm making my breakfast first." Lance reached for the bacon.

Aaron snatched the package away. "You can wait."

Gina entered the kitchen, saw the menacing looks on both their faces, and left.

Lance stared after her. Sure enough it hadn't taken her long to break. If she'd gone to the bunker at all.

He and Aaron exchanged a glance.

Aaron shrugged and turned on the stove. Smugness coated his face.

Lance felt his fingers curl, then forced down his anger. Fisticuffs with Aaron would be far different from fighting with Shari.

He took a deep breath and went to the fridge for bread. Flung two pieces in the toaster.

"*What* did you do to Shari?" Tori's accusing voice made Lance turn. She stood in the doorway.

"What's it to you?"

"Did you force your way into her room?"

"Why would I do that?"

"You tell me."

Lance leaned against the counter. "How about first you tell me about your stay in the *mental ward*?"

Tori recoiled.

Aaron laughed. He broke an egg into the pan.

"A sensitive topic, perhaps?" Lance cocked his head at Tori.

She eyed him. "You heard the clues from yesterday?"

"Why wouldn't I?"

"You weren't *here*."

"Right you are. I was … somewhere else. Receiving extra clues about *you*, as a matter of fact."

Tori's chin slowly rose. "Really. Do tell. Because I'd say you missed a great deal, not being in this house most of yesterday. Even if you did hear the clues."

Lance maintained a poker face. True, he'd missed interactions between people here. However he'd learned a few facts of his own in the bunker.

But so had Shari and Aaron.

"Care to discuss this in private, Tori?"

"Not in a *bedroom*, if that's what you're thinking."

Lance gave her a patronizing smile. "How about on the front deck?"

"Why should I want to be anywhere near you, after what you just did to Shari?"

"Because you want to win as much as I."

"Maybe you'll attack me."

"I expended my anger on Shari. You'll be safe."

No response.

"Out on the deck, Tori. Two minutes."

She gave him the eye, then made an event of leaving the kitchen.

Hah. He *had* her.

Lance pulled out his toast and covered the pieces thickly with butter and jam. Aaron had broken four eggs into the pan and was cooking bacon in the microwave.

"Quadruple eggs, Aaron? Think that's enough?"

He threw Lance a hard look. "As if you should talk. And if you'll remember, I didn't eat much yesterday."

Neither had Lance. He picked up his plate of toast. "For an attenuate man, you sure can devour food. I expect to find some eggs and bacon left when I get back."

He strode from the kitchen and into the great room.

Gina was perched in an armchair as close to the far corner as she could get. Lance halted and stared at her. She glanced up and caught his eye. Gina drew her head back like a threatened turtle. "What are *you* looking at?"

Lance raised his eyebrows. "Have a nice night?"

"Fine. Leave me alone."

Lance didn't move.

Gina made a sound in her throat. "What is *wrong* with you?"

Ah, playing demure in front of the cameras. Lance gave her a slow smile. "Hope you enjoyed yourself, vote winner."

He turned away, feeling her eyes still on him, and crossed the great room. Stepped outside on the deck. Tori sat a table, her back to him, head bent over her notebook.

Lance took the chair opposite her and set down his plate. His nerves shimmied. *Take control, man.*

"So." He indulged in a large bite of toast. "Why are we here?"

"I believe *you* called this meeting." Tori sounded almost bored. Lance wasn't buying it.

"Ah, yes." He paused for another bite.

Tori pushed back her chair. "You're wasting my time."

"Sit." Lance waved his half-eaten toast at her. "We have twenty minutes before the next set of clues."

Tori sighed, then clunked her chair back to the table. "Start talking."

Lance tossed the piece of toast on his plate. "Once again I propose a contract of mutual interest. I tell you something, you tell me something."

Silence.

"Agreed?"

"Depends on what you tell me."

Lance leaned forward and lowered his voice. "I know what Shari's secret is."

Tori tapped her chin. "I'd rather hear about you."

"Specifically what?"

"Who was the defendant at that trial, and how were you involved?"

"Who says I was involved?"

"The clues are about you."

"They're about Bruce, the man I interviewed, remember? We had this conversation during our last agreement."

And Tori had turned the tables on him, too. Lance wasn't about to forget that. At least now he knew what he'd wanted to learn then—Tori's illness had been a nervous breakdown.

Tori leaned back and folded her arms. "My questions stand. If you don't answer them, I tell you nothing."

"You haven't even heard what I want to know yet."

Tori gave him a slow blink.

"I want to know two things, since you're asking me two questions. What criminal act did Gina commit with her client? And what illegal business did *you* conduct with one of your younger male consorts?

Tori frowned. "What makes you think Gina or I did anything illegal?"

Ah, playing coy.

"And as far as your question about Gina, you'll have to ask her."

"Drop the pretense, Tori." Lance's tone hardened. He took a bite of toast, giving himself time to regroup. "Tell you what, I'll answer your questions first, in good faith. Then you answer mine."

She raised a hand—*go ahead.*

Lance's voice fell to a whisper. He could only hope the camera couldn't pick up his words. "The defendant was Richard Glass. He stole money from the company he worked for, which happened to be the same company Bruce worked for after his graduation from rehab. I hadn't talked to Bruce since I interviewed him, but when I heard he was being brought in to testify against his co-worker, I was concerned. Would the stress make him fall back into using? So I reached out as an encouragement." Lance shrugged. "That's the extent of it."

"Sure it is." Tori's words dripped with sarcasm. "You get docked points for lying, remember?"

"It's true."

"So what did *you* do wrong? What's your 'secret'?"

Lance's gaze drifted through the windows into the great room. Craig had come in and was talking to Gina. A sliver of panic thrust into Lance's chest. Another conversation he wasn't privy to, more information exchanged that he could not hear. He had to learn it all, be everywhere at once. How was he going to *do* this?

"Hey." Tori's fingernail tapped the table.

Lance forced himself to refocus. He glanced at the camera. "I fear we may be overheard."

"Write it down."

He hesitated, then tore a piece of paper from his notebook and wrote.

I knew Bruce before he went into rehab. I bought drugs for him on three occasions and used with him.

Lance turned the paper over and slid it across the table to Tori. She pulled it close and read.

Tori looked up and eyed Lance, as if trying to decide if he was telling the truth.

Lance snatched the piece of paper back, folded it and stuck it in his notebook. He would destroy it the first moment he could.

Tori leaned back in her chair, still studying him.

"All right, I've kept my promise. Now you answer my two questions."

One side of Tori's mouth curved. "Fine. Gina and her client falsified documents about a house. And I and a 'consort' held up a bank."

Lance tilted his head. "*You*, rob a bank? I find that hard to believe."

Tori pushed back her chair. "My answers are as reliable as yours." With a contemptuous smile, she picked up her notebook and stalked away.

Chapter 37

After psycho Lance stormed from her room, Shari threw herself on the bed and sobbed. First all the horrid clues about something she'd done in one weak moment. Then being tortured in a dungeon and told she'd *die* unless she confessed. Now she was back at the house—but was she safe? Oh, no. She couldn't even open her door without being attacked!

This show could not end fast enough. If she didn't win, everyone else involved—and she meant *everyone*—would see her in court.

And by the way, she'd thought *Aaron* may be Wrath? Not anymore. Lance was.

If Lance was Wrath, then Aaron had to be Pride.

She sniffed.

Hey, wait. She was getting somewhere. She already knew Gina was Gluttony, Tori was Lust, and she, herself, was nothing. That just left Craig.

Shari's tears stopped. She wiped her face. Enough crying. She was sick of ruining her makeup.

She turned on her back, staring at the ceiling. She needed to win the most votes announcement at noon—the last one. And she had to figure out who Craig was—

Sloth, Greed, or Envy. Probably Greed. He'd stolen a lot of money.

Today she'd hear two more clues about Craig. After that, she'd know what sin he was. She'd run to her room and be the first to lock in her answers.

How about that, George Fry. Thought you could stop Shari Steele?

She could still win this thing.

Shari checked her watch. Yikes. Only fifteen minutes to fix the mess she'd made of her makeup and hair.

She ran to the bathroom and put drops in her eyes to erase the redness. Cleaned up her face and brushed her hair. Then checked herself in the bathroom's full length mirror. She looked good. Great, in fact. At least Lance hadn't torn her clothes. Her tight green shirt matched her eyes, and the white shorts were perfect against her tan. She added a thin gold bracelet on her right wrist, and a long chain necklace. Now all she needed were her bling green sandals.

Shari slipped them on her feet and threw a kiss at the mirror.

Head high and a confident expression plastered on her face, she mounted the stairs five minutes before nine o'clock. Her notebook felt slick in her sweaty palms.

The other contestants had already gathered in the great room. No one spoke. So much love in this place. Sunshine and ocean breeze outside? Who noticed? The room felt as dark and heavy as the bunker.

Shari stole a look at Gina. Had she been to that death trap and back already? What on earth illegal thing had *she* done? Had to be more than having an affair with some client. Gina tried to come off looking so scared and helpless. It was the quiet ones you could never trust.

Hope your night was terrifying. And long.

The clock's big hand reached nine.

Shari's pulse skipped. She could feel a vein throb in her neck. Clamping on a smile, she prayed the clue about her would be an easy one. She'd already confessed. What more damage could they do to her?

Light played across the screen, and the *Dream Prize* logo appeared. Shari set her jaw and opened her notebook.

DREAM PRIZE

<u>Tuesday 9 a.m.</u>

In early February 2014, *Gina* told her former client she would not be seeing him again.

~~~

On January 9, 2014, *Craig's* accountant did not show up for work.

~~~

On January 8, 2014, after dinner with his mother, *Aaron* hit a pole as he drove his rental car into the hotel's parking garage.

~~~

From May through August 2012, Kathryn Flex, *Shari's* roommate at the time, recuperated from her attack.

~~~

In December 2012 *Lance's* son, Scott, changed jobs, vacationing in the Caribbean before starting his new position.

~~~

In June 2002, *Tori's* divorce was finalized.

Chapter 38

Heart skidding, Craig finished writing the list of clues in his notebook and moved away from the monitor. He stared at the words about himself, reliving the day over two years ago when an employee reported that Nate hadn't shown up for work. Again. Nate had been so reliable when Craig hired him. Until Tori Hattinger got her hooks in him. She'd lifted Nate up—and let go. Crashed him to the pavement.

On that morning of January 9, 2014, Craig had known what his employees did not. Nate would never again return to his job.

Craig took a deep breath. One more set of clues, one more day to go. What if something happened? What if he couldn't keep his biggest 'secret' hidden?

His life would be *done*.

Craig's gaze moved over the other contestants. They were still writing. Gina's mouth pinched, her lowered head folding the fat beneath her chin. Tori held her notebook a little too tightly with those chic, manicured hands. Defiance marched across Shari's face. That girl. She never stopped acting. Aaron gave off his typical wooden look. Lance was breathing too hard, air seeping in and out of his big throat.

Tori closed her notebook, looked up and caught Craig's eye. "*Why?*" she mouthed.

Was she talking about his clue? How dare *she* ask anything about Nate. "Why what?"

She shook her head.

"Oh. You don't want to speak of it out in the open, is that it? I assume you're asking why my accountant didn't come to work."

Lance, Shari, and Aaron glanced from him to Tori, their expressions questioning.

"Go ahead, Tori." Craig lifted his hand. "Tell them what we're talking about. They missed the show yesterday."

She gave him a look to kill.

"What's he talking about?" Shari asked.

"Nothing."

"Yes, he is."

Tori's neck reddened. "Fine, keep at me, Shari. See if I come to your defense next time you're attacked."

"You didn't exactly help!"

"You didn't exactly *let* me."

Shari pushed air through her teeth. "I didn't need your help. I don't need help from *any* of you!"

She and Tori glared at each other.

Craig turned to Aaron. "Weird fact about *you*, hitting that pole in your rental car. Too mad to drive straight?"

Aaron smirked. "Nice try, but we're talking about *your* clue. Why didn't your accountant come to work?"

Craig's eyes shifted meaningfully to Tori. "He was depressed, if you must know. Heartsick."

Aaron followed Craig's gaze, frowning. Craig could practically see the calculations in his head.

"Wait a minute," Gina said. "What's this about someone attacking Shari?"

"You telling me you didn't hear the noise? It was *Lance*." Shari spat the name. "And that was the *second* time."

"And behold her perfection now." Lance dragged down the corners of his mouth. "Not a hair out of place. Some victim."

Tori smacked her notebook on the table. "Know what? I find it beyond comprehension that all three men here have attacked all three women at one time or another." She stared daggers at Craig, then Aaron. "Is *this* what you do in your normal lives? Who in the world taught you to act like that? Where were your mothers?"

Aaron's face blackened. "*Don't* you talk about my mother."

"Yeah, you don't want to mess with *him*," Craig said. "Just ask Gina."

Tori's eyes narrowed. "I don't recall your treating me any better, Craig. *You* knocked me to the ground."

"As if you didn't deserve it."

"See? That's just what I mean. If a woman is mistreated, it's *her* fault. Never the man's. He's always got good reason."

But it was all right for *her* to mistreat *men*? Craig thought. "You need to quit talking, Tori. You think you're so great? Worked your way up in life after your husband divorced you? Good for you. So you'd think you would have more empathy for others. But you've got *none*."

Tori drew her head back like a snake set to strike.

"You want to hit me, go ahead." Craig turned his cheek toward her and patted it. "Right here. Show the people out there what you're really like."

Lance laughed. "She just might, too."

"*Do* it, Tori," Gina said.

Tori's glittering eyes turned on her. "I don't need any help from an *adulterer*." She snatched her notebook off the table and strutted from the room.

"I am *not* an adulterer!"

"Don't go away mad!" Craig called after Tori. "Just go away!"

Lance guffawed.

Gina pursed her mouth. "You're disgusting people, *all* of you." She turned her back and headed for the deck.

Craig watched her go.

Well, now, look who was left in the room—the four happy bunker mates. He gestured with his chin toward Gina. "Do you think she went ...? After she won the votes yesterday?"

Lance shrugged. "Anybody see her last night after the announcement?"

Three shaking heads.

"You'd think she'd be quaking in her metaphorical boots if she did."

"Yeah." Craig nodded. "Totally."

"But why *shouldn't* she have to go?" Shari's eyes flashed. "That's not *fair*."

Craig surveyed her. What a base human being. If something bad happened to Shari Steele, it had to happen to everybody.

Aaron turned and walked away without a word.

"Hey, wait." Lance went after him. "We need to talk."

"No we don't."

Their voices faded.

Shari looked at Craig. "And I need to talk to *you*."

Well, this should be fun. "Fine. I want to sit down." He walked to a sofa in the corner and sank into it. Shari took a seat in an armchair, facing him. "So." Craig tossed his notebook on the couch. "What do you want?"

"I'm trying to make sense of your clues." Shari strategically tucked her hair behind one ear.

"And why should I help you?"

"Because I'll help you back."

"Really. What could you possibly do for me?"

She lifted a hand. "Who do you want to know about? I must have a piece of information you need."

Craig considered the floor, picturing his hysterical bunker confession. "What more could you need to know about me? You already heard more than you should."

"Yeah, but how does that fit with your clues?"

Craig shrugged.

"The last four have been about some accountant. Who cares?"

"Maybe I do. Maybe he was a good guy."

"*Was?*"

If she only knew. "Figure of speech."

Shari looked at Craig from the corner of her eye. "Really."

"That was my line, Shari, did you forget yours?"

"This isn't a script."

"Of course it is. Everything's a script with you. Isn't that what you want—to be some Hollywood star?"

Her black fingernails dug into the chair. "This is not about me, it's about *you.*"

"You said you'd give me something in return."

"I want your answer first."

"Oh. Right."

Shari crossed her legs, sliding her feet to one side. Perfect lengthening angle for the camera. "So, Craig—your '*was*' accountant. Does he still work for you?"

Craig drew a bored breath. "No."

"Did you fire him?"

"No."

"Did he quit?"

Craig looked away.

"*Did* he quit?"

Craig smacked both hands against the edge of the couch and stood. "We're done here."

"No!" Shari jumped up. "Wait, just hear me out."

He picked up his notebook. "Know what? Here's something interesting. *Your* last four clues haven't been about *you*, either. They've been about your ex roommate, Kathryn Flex. Somebody very famous now, thanks to her debut movie. What a rocket to fame. I'll bet you're really happy for her. *Aren't* you?"

Shari's cheeks hardened. If the cameras weren't on, she'd have slapped him.

Craig gave a slow nod. "Just as I thought."

He turned and left the room.

Chapter 39

Aaron lurked in the hall around the corner from the great room. He'd gotten rid of Lance in time to circle back and hear the last of Craig's and Shari's conversation.

Footsteps from the room approached.

Aaron darted for the stairs. He didn't stop until he'd slipped into his bedroom and locked the door. He flung himself into his desk chair.

Think.

He ran the clues about Craig's accountant through his head.

January 8, 2014—the guy went out to dinner with friends. Who? Craig? Not at work the next day. Craig said because he was depressed.

Was he lying?

The guy didn't work for Craig anymore. Why?

What if he *never returned to work*?

Aaron dug fingers into his scalp.

He swiveled around and stared at his yacht photograph on the wall. *Lisa.* He *had* to win for Lisa.

A minute later, notebook open, Aaron was writing like mad. Drawing circles. Making connections …

By the time he raised his head it was almost noon. Panic spritzed his nerves. Time for the final announcement of the most votes winner.

It had to be him.

Aaron hurried from his room and locked the door, leaving his notebook behind.

Chapter 40

This round's majority of votes go to Tori Hattinger.

Tori went nearly faint with relief.

She could hear the hissed breaths around her. So much animosity pulsing and swirling the air. At the moment she didn't care. She'd *done* it! Her time spent talking to viewers this morning had paid off.

All her votes today would double.

Tori smiled at a camera. "Thank you, everyone. Thank you so much."

"Why?" Aaron sneered. "What did *you* do to win?"

Ah, poor Aaron—the only person who'd never won. And this had been his last chance.

"Don't act too spiteful." She wagged a finger at him. "Votes are still coming in until three o'clock. Maybe you'll pick up one or two before then."

She threw him a catty smile and headed out of the room for her extra clue.

"Careful!" Craig called. "Wouldn't want anything bad happening to you."

Uh-huh. Just because *he'd* disappeared into who-knew-where. No way she'd fall for that.

Tori's sandals clicked as she trotted down the stairs. In her bedroom she switched on her camera.

The green light glowed.

She sat in her chair. *Easy, Tori. Be calm.* "Hello again." She swallowed. "I want to know the name of the trial defendant mentioned in Lance's clues."

Tori focused on her monitor, waiting.

Waiting.

Come on.

The monitor lit up. Tori leaned forward.

That question has already been asked and answered. Choose another one.

What? She'd been trying to learn that information for *two days*.

Tori swung back to the camera. "Ask another question? That's not fair! When was *this* new rule made?"

Her gaze fixed again on the monitor. The words faded, replaced by new text.

You have two minutes.

Air gushed from Tori's mouth. Two minutes? She didn't have a backup question. Never dreamed she'd need one.

She flung open her notebook, poring over her writing. Feeling the seconds tick away. A muscle in the back of her neck began to twitch.

Wait, what was she *thinking*? Of course she knew what to ask.

"Okay, okay!" She tossed her words at the camera. "I want to know about Craig's accountant. Why didn't he show up for work?"

Tori watched the monitor.

"He was depressed." Craig's words echoed in her head. Uneasiness seeped into her veins. She thought of her own depression all those years ago, her own reason for not going to work that day ...

New text materialized on the screen.

He was in the hospital.

Tori stared at the words, then sagged against the back of her chair. Heat swept over her face.

The hospital?

Steady, girl. Viewers were ogling her like witnesses at a freak accident.

She tilted her head toward the hungry lens. "The answer says he was in the hospital." Tori forced a little smile. "I'll talk to you later."

Her hand reached up and turned off the camera.

Guilt washed over Tori like dirty water. She'd done this to Nate, who never deserved it. He'd been in love with her. Had asked her to marry him. And her break-up with him apparently left him so depressed he'd attempted *suicide?* Just like she'd done after her husband rejected her.

Tori shoved away from the desk and stood. Paced across the room.

She could not bear knowing this. It was too much.

She strode to the closed curtains. To the bathroom. The bed. Back to the curtains.

Wait a minute. *Wait.*

Her legs halted.

This wasn't fair. What Nate did wasn't her fault. It had been *his* choice. They'd only dated four months. They weren't married like she and Merrill had been. She'd never pledged Nate her life. He should have pulled himself together.

Nate was weak. This proved it. Good thing she'd walked away from him.

Tori's eyes stung with tears. Still, wherever Nate was now, she hoped he'd found strength. That he was happy.

Tears fell. Tori wiped them away with impatience. This was not the time for *her* to be weak. She had less than three hours to solve this game.

She walked to the bathroom and drank a glass of water. Methodically fixed her makeup.

As the minutes ticked by she felt her resolve return.

When she was done, Tori checked herself in the mirror. Pronounced herself ready.

Taking a deep breath, she picked up her notebook and left the room.

Chapter 41

Two hours and forty minutes left.

Gina gripped the deck railing. Her body felt numb. So much to figure out and so little time. Where to even start? Meanwhile she could *feel* the viewers watching her. Salivating over her every facial expression. They wanted to see her hurting, lost, nearly beside herself with worry. They couldn't wait for the next argument between contestants, maybe a knock-down, drag-out fight.

She could not leave this island soon enough.

But what kind of life would she return to? Would Ben *believe* her?

Even if he did, she'd be caught in her lies forever. Another sin on her conscience, acting as a barrier between herself and God. She could ask Jesus again for mercy and forgiveness. But then she'd have to stop lying, tell Ben the truth. How could she do that?

God, what do you expect of me? Why are You letting this happen?

Gina turned toward the house. She'd deal with those after-the-show problems later. Right now she had to talk to viewers in her bedroom. Again. Deny the latest clue. Again.

She hurried through the great room and swerved into the hall, nearly knocking into Lance.

"Oh!" She pulled back.

"Where are you going, I have to talk to you." Lance's hands fidgeted, sweat on his temples. He looked like someone about to topple off a cliff.

"I don't want to talk to *you*." Gina tried to push around him.

Lance thrust out his hand to block her. Gina froze. This man had reportedly attacked Shari twice. "Get away from me."

"Answer one question."

"No."

"Come on, Gina."

"*No*."

Footsteps clacked up the stairs. Someone was in a hurry. Tori appeared, took one look at the two of them and halted.

"What's going on?"

"He won't let me go!" Panic coated Gina's voice. She pictured Ben watching, heart in his throat. Wondering if he could still believe in her.

She *had* to get to her room.

"Lance, *stop* it." Tori punched his arm. "You're nothing but a big bully."

He jerked around, towering over her, his face dark red. "Mind your own business, Tori!"

"This *is* my business! What do you want?"

"For you to leave. *Now*."

Gina cringed away from both of them. "Whatever you want me to tell you, Lance—the answer is still no." She moved toward the stairs.

Lance caught her arm and hung on. "Wait."

"Let go of me!" She tried to pull away.

"Listen, *please*." Lance's mouth hung open as he dragged in air. The guy really looked like he was losing it. "We can help each other."

Tori's eyebrows rose. "Oh? And what about me?"

Gina threw her a look. So much for the woman's true colors. Tori didn't care what Lance did to her. She didn't care for anybody but herself.

"Let go of my arm right now, Lance."

Aaron appeared from the kitchen. He stopped and leaned against the doorway, watching intently, as if some valuable piece of information might be exchanged here.

"Okay," Lance said. "But hear me out." He loosened his fingers.

Gina stared daggers at him, tucking her arm by her side. "*What?*"

Lance gestured with his head toward the great room. "Outside."

"Don't fall for it, Gina." Tori scoffed. "This man's nothing but lies."

"No, really. No time for that now." Lance sounded almost pleading.

If he wanted to barter information, it was too late. Gina already knew what sin Lance represented.

Aaron laughed. "Look at the big guy, falling apart."

"I wouldn't talk, Aaron." Lance glared at him. "You're the one who threw yourself at the door. Hurled a chair across the room."

When was this? Gina frowned.

Aaron bristled. "Keep at it, Lance, disqualify yourself from the game."

"I've got things to do." Gina pivoted toward the stairs.

"No, wait," Tori called. "I was coming up to see you."

Lance lumbered after Gina and clapped a hand on her shoulder.

She whirled on him. "How stupid *are* you? I *don't* want to talk!"

He leaned in close. Gina could smell salami on his breath. "We could unite our efforts," he said in her ear. "Double each other's chance of winning."

"Ignore whatever he's telling you," Tori said. "Talk to me instead."

Gina's gaze bounced from Lance to Tori. "I just want to go to my room."

"*Double chances*, Gina," Lance whispered.

"How?"

He glanced at Tori, who was watching them like a hawk. "Not here."

"I'm not going anywhere alone with you."

"I promise I won't touch you again." Lance held up both hands.

"Lies, lies." Tori tossed her head.

"Shut *up*!" Lance chopped his hand through the air.

"See what I mean, Gina? He's dangerous."

Lance's fingers curled. He pulled up straight, visibly trying to steady himself. A drop of sweat plinked into his eyes.

He motioned toward the lower floor. "I'll walk down with you."

Fine, anything to just get closer to her room. Gina would run for its safety, lock the door.

She nodded.

"Gina, no!" Tori threw out her hand. "We've got to talk, there's not much time."

What *was* this? Why was Gina Corrales so important all of a sudden?

"Later, Tori."

"We don't *have* much 'later!'"

The walls were tightening around Gina. She had to get away from these people. "Tori, I said *no*." She started down the stairs as fast as she could. Lance clomped after her.

Gina hit the bottom floor and kept going, swerving around the corner into the bedroom hallway.

"Stop." Lance drew up beside her, panting.

No way did she have time to run inside her room before he would try to block her. Indignation shot through Gina. This had gone far enough.

She straightened her back. "*What* do you want? And make it fast."

How the viewers must love this.

Lance swallowed. "I *can't* lose."

"Not my problem."

"Neither can you."

"What's that to you? You don't know hardly anything about me."

"You're right. But I have information I gathered while I was ... gone. Facts about Shari and Craig and Aaron. You know what happened here. *I* know what happened there. We exchange that information. Also exchange other facts we've discovered. Become a team. If one of us wins, we split the ten million."

Gina pulled her head back. Was this guy crazy?

"Gina, it's a good plan. You'd have twice the chance of winning. Five million is still a lot of money. Enough to fulfill your dream, I'll bet."

Gina's eyes searched the floor. Enough? Not after she'd set her sights on *ten* million. Still ...

"Why me, Lance? Why don't you team up with somebody else?"

"Because you're only one of two people who were here the whole time."

"So—Tori."

"Tori hates me."

With good reason. Gina shook her head. "No way."

"Please. *Think* about it."

"There's nothing to think about. First of all, why in the world would I trust you to share the prize if you won?"

"We'll draw up a contract and sign it. In front of the cameras."

Right.

"Lance, I'm a realtor, I know all about contracts. Even if such a document held up in court, we'd be fighting over the money for years. Believe me, the last thing I want is to see any of you people again."

Desperation rolled across his face. "You wouldn't have to fight me. I'd give you the money."

Tori was right. This man was full of lies.

But he also had information she could use.

"I'm not teaming up with you, signing a contract with you — or *anything*." Gina looked up at Lance. "But I am willing to exchange some information."

"What can you tell me?"

"Some of the clues we heard yesterday."

"I already have yesterday's clues."

"You do?"

"Tell me something else. Like why that affair you had with Aaron's father is so important."

Gina blanched. "*What*? *Where* did you get that? I never had an affair. With *anyone*!"

"That's what the clues said."

"They *never* said that, it's merely your assumption. And even if they had, it would be a lie!"

"Then you had an affair with some other client."

"I did not!"

Lance's head tilted. "Gina, I know you did, and somehow it led to illegal conduct. I can't tell you my information if you won't be honest with me."

"I *am* being honest.'"

"Then what? All those clues about you—they're just lies? Where does that leave us?"

Fine, he wanted to play this game? Gina would give it right back to him. "Here's what *I* want to know, Lance. Who is Douglas West?"

Lance froze. "Where did you hear that name?"

"My extra clue. How were you involved in his trial?"

"I wasn't."

"Your clues said you were."

"No they didn't. That's just your assumption."

"Like *your* assumption is that I had some affair?"

Lance pressed his big face close to hers. "You *did*."

"Then *you* were involved in that trial."

Lance started to say something, then closed his mouth. He straightened, his neck reddening. "I hope you *lose*, Gina."

He stomped toward the stairs, smacking the wall on his way.

Chapter 42

One-thirty. Half an hour before the last clues.

Craig sat in his bedroom, nerves prickling. This thing was almost over. He couldn't wait to get out of the house, away from these people. It was bad enough before, but since noon the place had gone totally crazy. Everyone was running around, slinging long-shot "deals," practically trying to slap information out of each other.

At this point he just needed to keep calm. Keep telling himself he would win.

After the clues they'd have one hour to lock in their answers.

Craig could imagine what the other five disgusting contestants were doing right now. They were agonizing over which of the Seven Deadly Sins matched to each person, praying that the final set of clues would erase any doubt from their minds. After those last clues, they'd run to lock in their answers as soon as possible. Because in case of a tie, whoever locked in first would win.

He needed to make his own list. He needed to be ready.

Before three and four o'clock, the house should go silent. Finally. Everyone would be packing. Waiting. Then at four—the winner announcement.

Craig broke out in a cold sweat. So much rested on these next few hours. He would be the victor here. He *would*.

He walked into the bathroom and splashed his face with cold water.

Back at his desk, he pulled the picture of his niece from his wallet. Ran a finger over her smiling face.

Looking at Annie always inspired him.

Reverently, Craig replaced the photo.

He opened his notebook to a fresh page and began to write.

Craig's Notebook

Gina: Lust

Me: none

Aaron: Pride

Shari: Envy

Lance: Gluttony

Tori: Greed

Chapter 43

One forty-five.

Lance paced his room. His notebook lay open on the desk, waiting for him to make his semifinal list. But try as he might, he couldn't do it.

So many questions remained. And the stakes were mind-numbingly high. Unless the final clues laid it out in black and white, he would be doomed.

His *son* would be doomed.

Lance dropped his face in his hands, remembering his own fifth clue. It hadn't even focused on him. It had focused on Scott. His Caribbean vacation.

George Fry was honing in on them both. Dropping the facts one at a time, like plinking rocks in a pond.

And the final clue regarding Lance Haslow's sin? How bad would it be?

Lance checked his watch again. One-fifty.

A vise gripped his heart. Ten minutes left to get upstairs for the last clues. He had to make his tentative list —*now.*

He sat down hard in his chair and reached for his pen.

Gina: Gluttony (heavy woman)

Craig: Greed (embezzlement)
Aaron: Wrath (often angry)
Shari: Pride (killed her mother so she could return to Hollywood)
Me: N/A
Tori: Lust (multiple relationships with men)

Lance looked over the list. His uncertainty remained as strong, but how to change his answers? What better could he do?

He could only hope the final clues about others would bring clarity.

Please, God, if You're up there ...

Lance dragged to his feet and picked up his notebook. He could hardly feel his legs as he mounted the stairs. Gina, Craig, and Shari were already in the great room, looking frazzled. Lance joined them in a semicircle around the monitor, his heart chugging like a weak engine.

No one spoke.

Aaron entered. Followed by Tori.

The monitor began to lighten.

Tuesday 2 p.m.

In July 2014, after the divorce of her former client was final, *Gina* served as realtor to the client in his purchase of a condo and visited him there.

~~~

On January 13, 2014, a funeral was held for *Craig's* accountant.

~~~

On January 9, 2014, *Aaron* turned in his damaged rental car and flew back to his home in Austin, TX.

~~~

In June 2012, *Shari* left California, leaving injured Kathryn Flex without a roommate and unable to pay for their apartment alone.

~~~

In December 2012, *Lance* joined his son in the Caribbean for a two-week vacation.

~~~

In June 2014, *Tori* rejected a marriage proposal from a man twelve years her junior and soon began dating someone else.

Chapter 44

Shari stared at the monitor, her blood boiling.

"That clue about me is totally unfair!" She jabbed her finger at a camera. "It's not like I ditched Kathryn on purpose. I had to go home and nurse my mom. She was sick with cancer!"

Aaron snickered. "Aren't you Miss Goody Girl."

"*Shut* up, Aaron."

Shari clamped her teeth together and forced herself to *think*. She scribbled down the clues. Everyone else was writing, too.

She stared at her notebook, mind spinning. Trying to make final connections.

Overweight Gina went back to her affair—so what? She was still Gluttony. Craig's accountant died. Sad for whoever he was, but it didn't change Craig from being Greed. He'd stolen money.

Aaron went home to Texas. Poor boy, having to leave his mommy. Aaron was still Pride.

Shari Steele was still *nothing*.

Lance went on vacation in the Caribbean. Good for him. Maybe for a couple weeks he actually didn't attack anybody. Or maybe he took his Wrath out on every waiter who served him.

Tori dumped one sucker boyfriend for another. Lust and more Lust.

Hey.

Shari's head bounced up. Her list hadn't changed. She *had* it!

She ran out of the great room, sandals clicking.

Chapter 45

Tori read the second clue and felt her veins go cold.

No. No, no.

Nate *died?*

Why?

He'd been in the hospital after his suicide attempt. He was supposed to be *all right.* How could he have died? Was it a pill overdose? Maybe somebody found him, and he hung on for awhile, then fell into a coma.

Tori gripped her pen until her fingers cramped. She wanted to throw up.

She glanced at Craig. He was writing, his breaths ragged, as if he was about to explode with rage.

I didn't do it! she wanted to scream at him. *It wasn't my fault!*

Craig smacked his notebook shut and looked up. He caught Tori's eye and stared lasers at her.

"Don't," she spat.

Aaron looked from her to Craig.

Lance was writing, his hand shaking. Gina looked like she was in her own world.

A sudden, stunning realization hit Tori in the chest.

Wait.

All of these clues about Nate—they had to be based on Craig, not her. Right? She'd been too focused on herself. So what had *Craig* done to cause Nate's death?

That was it. Had to be. *Craig* had killed him.

Tori's blood ran cold.

The man was certainly capable. And somehow he rationalized it all, didn't he. And he continued to view himself above everyone else.

Tori's throat tightened. "What did you do to him, Craig?"

"What did *I* do?"

Rage coiled in her head. He'd done something, all right—just look at his face! Tori saw herself shaking the smug man, making him tell her the truth. But the other clues remained, and time was ticking, and she had to write the list in her notebook, and go, go, *go!* Get to her room, double check her list of sins, smack on the camera, announce she was ready to solve the game. Shari was already running out the door, heading to lock in her answers first—

Heart pounding, Tori shifted her eyes back to the clues. Forced herself to concentrate on writing.

When she got to her own clue, it took everything she had not to sweep the monitor to the floor and smash it. What she did in her personal life was her *own business*!

Done with her writing, Tori spun on her heel and strode for the stairs.

In her room she skimmed over the list she'd made less than half an hour ago. She still wasn't sure about all her choices. But she was a business executive. This was what she did—made the best decisions she could under pressure.

Tori punched on her camera.

"I am ready to solve the game."

Her throat ran dry. Tori swallowed.

"In order of the clues, here are my answers. "Gina is Lust. Craig is Pride. Aaron is Wrath. Shari is Envy. Lance is Greed. I am no sin."

Chapter 46

Tears ran down Gina's face as she wrote. That last clue about herself! *Why?* Yes, she'd seen Shan again—after she'd told him the affair was over. He'd needed a realtor, and she wanted the money. She was always looking to make more money. So what? She hadn't *meant* to be with him again personally, it just *happened*. And after that visit to his condo, she *did* stop seeing him—for *good*. That was almost two years ago.

How did George Fry know all this? And what business was it of his? It was after seeing Shan that last time that Gina had asked God for forgiveness. Then she'd moved on. Nobody had a right to judge her past mistakes, not when God had wiped them clean. Nobody had a right to *ruin her marriage!*

The tears ran off her chin. Gina wiped them away. How she must look on camera.

When she finished writing, she looked up at the viewers, mouth trembling.

"It's not true, Ben. I don't know why they're doing this to me."

"Stop *lying!*" Aaron's cheeks turned brick red. He shoved his finger against her chest. "*You* did it. *You!*"

"No! I just sold him a house!"

Aaron threw his notebook down and raised both hands toward Gina's neck. She screamed.

"Whoa, stop!" Craig jumped toward Aaron and dragged him backward.

"Get out of here, Gina!" Aaron fought to free himself. "Get out of my sight!"

Gina whirled and ran for safety.

She pounded down the stairs, breathing erratically, and veered into the hallway. Her hand trembled so hard she couldn't get her bedroom key into the lock. Finally the door swung open. She leapt inside and slammed the door. Turned the bolt.

She leaned against the door, mouth open, sucking in air.

Think, think.

This was it, no more time. She had to lock in her answers. Shari and Tori might have already beat her to it.

Gina flung herself into the desk chair and slapped through her notebook. She'd learned little in the last set of clues. Except that Tori's clue was about yet another relationship. That made three. The clues were showing a pattern. Tori was Lust.

As for Aaron—he was Wrath. Gina had known that since yesterday.

Shari? Pride. She oozed it.

Lance was Gluttony.

And, of course, Gina herself was nothing.

What about Craig?

Sloth, maybe? Because he may have inherited money from his parents. But even if he had, he still worked for his foundation—for no pay. How would that be Sloth?

Had he told the truth about his salary?

Gina squeezed her eyes shut. *Please, God, why won't You help me?*

Out of nowhere (God?) an arresting thought flashed through her brain. What if God *was* trying to help, and she hadn't been listening? What if, even in experiencing His mercy for her sin, there may still be consequences to pay? Would she be willing to do whatever God asked of her, walk in His truth? Or would she go her own way again?

The questions gripped Gina so tightly she couldn't move.

She shook her head hard. *Later.* Right now the clock ticked.

Time to finish this.

Gina took a long, deep breath, and forced her back to straighten. She turned on her camera. The green button lit up.

Her fists clenched. "I am ready to solve the game …"

Chapter 47

Aaron hurried into his bedroom and locked the door. He, Lance, and Craig had left the great room at the same time. All trying to get down the stairs first.

Aaron had beaten them.

He sat down, his mind popping. That last clue about Tori dating another man—it had to be important.

Could Tori be Lust?

Then what was Gina?

She *had* to be Lust. She'd broken up his parents' marriage.

So what was Tori?

Maybe Envy. She dated younger men. Maybe she wanted to be young herself.

Shari was Pride. Aaron knew that.

Craig was Greed. He'd stolen five million dollars.

Lance was Gluttony.

Aaron was nothing—

He sank his fingers into his cheeks. Wait. *He* knew he was none of the sins, but that's not what the clues about him pointed to. He had to look at this rationally.

Aaron squeezed his eyes shut. He pictured Lisa's face. The yacht. The future they could have.

He had to do this. Now.

But he had to get it right.

He lowered his head, brain clattering through possibilities ... probabilities ...

This game was not fair, had never been. The show would label him with some sin.

Aaron jerked up. He was ready.

He smacked on the camera.

"I am ready to solve the game. I'll start with myself. I am Wrath ..."

Chapter 48

Five minutes after three. In less than an hour Lance would hear his fate. Game winner and millionaire — or unable to fund his and Scott's lives on the run.

That last clue about himself had sealed their fate. He and his son could not stay in the U.S.

Lance lay on his bed, muscles quivering.

Despite his desperate prayer, the last set of clues had not helped him. And therefore his list of contestants and sins had not changed. He now second- and third-guessed his choices.

He'd done the best he could.

Now that his answers had been locked in, Lance felt … empty. No more information to extract from people like impacted teeth. No more alliances to scheme.

He had to win. And receive his money quickly. Before the police showed up at his door.

Lance stared at the ceiling, imagining his confession leaked to law enforcement. How soon would Fry do it?

Maybe he wouldn't. As Lance had surmised before, the man was simply a sadist.

But why *wouldn't* he, after going to such lengths to obtain those confessions? How long had it taken to dig that bunker?

Either way, released or not, Lance would forever know the tape was out there. Somewhere. Hanging over his neck like the sword of Damocles.

Lance buffed his face. He was driving himself crazy.

He hoisted to his feet to pack. Then halted.

His feet took him to the sliding door. For the first time, Lance pulled it and the curtains fully open. The sun shone in, and a fresh breeze blew over his face. He closed his eyes and concentrated on simply enjoying it.

Nature. Such beauty.

Lance turned away to fetch his suitcase from the closet. He threw it on the bed and tossed in clothes and toiletries, leaving his notebook on the desk. When he was finished he checked for anything he'd overlooked and closed the bag. He left it sitting by the open sliding door. No point in locking up anymore.

With one last look around the premises, he picked up his notebook and headed upstairs for something to eat.

Chapter 49

Five minutes to go.

Shari sat on the arm of a sofa in the great room, one leg bouncing.

Please, please, please.

Everybody else had gathered, just as antsy as she was. Nobody talked. They just paced and gripped their notebooks and threw hateful looks at each other.

Another minute of waiting, and Shari just might be sick. Her stomach was all knotty, and her back was sticky. So much for changing clothes before she'd packed. She wasn't even trying to hide her nervousness anymore. All viewer votes were in, so what difference did it make?

Now all she had to do was get through this winner announcement—*Shari Steele!*—and survive the boat ride back to the mainland with these horrible people. Who she *never* wanted to see again in her *entire life*.

She twisted around to check the big clock on the wall. Same as her watch. Two minutes left.

No need to worry. Truly. She had this. She'd gotten to her bedroom first to lock in her decisions. Even if she tied in correct answers with someone, she'd still win—

"Stop jiggling!" Craig hit the back of the couch. "You're shaking the floor."

Wow, look at him. Totally pasty. "So? It's a big floor, go to the other side."

One minute to four.

Shari stood and walked to the table in the center of the room. Her ankles were mushy. Memories of seeing the sets of clues washed over her, leaving her gritty. How she'd hated that vulnerable feeling. This was the last time she'd have to stand before this stupid monitor.

Tori drifted over, and Lance, and Aaron. Lance had been sitting out on the deck, chowing down on meat and cheese and potato chips. Gina's eyes were red. Tori and Aaron were both all stiff-faced, but Shari saw right through them. Aaron stuck his notebook under one arm and gripped his elbows, feet spread.

Four o'clock.

"Here we go," Lance said under his breath.

The monitor lit up. Shari's stomach turned over.

The Dream Prize logo appeared, then quickly faded, replaced with George Fry, sitting on his bare chair against a white background just like before.

Shari's eyes narrowed. *Monster. Torturer.*

Someday in Hollywood, after she was a big star, she would see George Fry somewhere. Maybe at a party or at the Oscars. She couldn't wait to spit in his face. When she got big enough and rich enough, she'd ruin the man.

"Greetings to all of you." Fry gave them one of his evil little smiles. "I trust you've had a pleasant three days."

Yeah, real pleasant. Especially in the bunker.

"Once we're done here, the boat captain will arrive to take you back to the mainland. You'll have to get your own suitcases to the boat, I'm afraid. As for the winner, I offer you my pre-congratulations. You will be contacted within two days of arriving home regarding your prize."

Fry shifted in his chair. "And now I bid my goodbye. Your judgment follows—pronouncing each person's representation of the Seven Deadly Sins. Only then will you see the winner's name."

The monitor went blank.

Shari pushed back her shoulders. Suddenly, the announcement of the winner seemed an eternity away. First they had to face "judgment"—from a man with no mercy. A man of pure evil himself. And there was nothing any of them could do to stop it.

Dread snaked through the room.

Shari hugged her arms to her chest.

Text appeared on the screen.

Gina has shown herself to never be satisfied with what she has. She wants more sales, more money, a bigger house. Worst of all, not content with her own loving husband, she wanted the husband of another woman. Gina Corrales is GREED.

What?

A low wail came out of Gina's throat.

"No way!" Shari glared at the monitor. "She's Gluttony. Look how fat she is!"

Craig's face twisted. "Man, Shari, that's so disgustingly shallow and wrong, even for *you.*"

"I'm not *either* of those things!" Gina cried. "How *dare* you, Shari."

"She had an affair with my father!" Aaron yelled at a camera. "She's Lust!"

"I am *not* shallow, Craig—" Shari clamped her mouth shut. What did Aaron say? His *father?*

Tears ran down Gina's cheeks. "This shouldn't be happening. I'm so sorry, Ben. I'm *so sorry.*"

"Oh, yeah, so sorry." Aaron wagged his head.

Gina and *Aaron's father?*

Something drew Shari's eyes to Tori. The woman did not look surprised at the news. But she also didn't seem very happy.

She'd guessed wrong, too.

Shari pressed her lips together. Maybe they'd all gotten this one wrong.

The words disappeared from the screen. Gina was still crying.

"Be *quiet!*" Tori flapped a hand at her.

New light came on the monitor. Followed by a close-up of Craig's face, looking all wild-eyed and crazy. Shari's blood turned cold. She'd seen Craig looking like that. *In the bunker.*

No, no, no.

"What?" Craig jerked toward the table. "No, you can't—"

His face onscreen came to life, air stuttering in and out of his mouth. "I embezzled m-money from my last job. At an ac-counting firm. Five million dollars. I used it to—start my f-foundation."

Craig's face stilled again, his mouth wide open, spittle on his lips. Across the bottom of the screen, text appeared.

Believing he was above the law, Craig viewed himself as the savior of others. Craig Emberly is PRIDE.

Nobody moved, all of them staring at the screen.

No, no, no, no, no. If they'd shown Craig's confession …

Gina hiccupped a sob. "Where did that come from?"

"Why did you *do* that?" Craig threw out his hands. "You *told* us you wouldn't! You— I'd have said anything to get out of there—you know it's all a lie!"

"Where *were* you?" Tori's eyes were round.

Lance and Aaron looked shell-shocked.

Shari wrenched herself together. "Wait a minute, George Fry, why is he Pride? He told you he stole money. That makes him *Greed*." She swung toward Gina and Craig. "This whole show is fixed. Who's some game producer to say what sin you two are? *I* say you're something else, and it *fits*. My judgment's just as good as anybody's!"

"Your judgment doesn't run this game." Tori looked so very happy with herself. "*I* got Craig right—without even knowing he embezzled money. He *acts* proud. All the time."

Craig's face contorted. "Who are *you* to say what I am?"

"And who are you to judge *anybody*, after what *you* did?" Tori pointed at his picture on the monitor. "When you get home, you're going to jail!"

Craig launched himself at Tori.

Lance jumped in his way and shoved him back. "Stop, the next one's coming!"

Craig scrambled sideways and shook himself off.

The screen was changing again, Craig fading out.

Shari dug fingers into her hair. She wanted to stop this, stop all of it. Everything was happening so fast. And it was all so wrong.

On the monitor, Craig turned into Aaron. His frozen face was a mask of hatred. Was this in the bunker, too?

Aaron saw his own picture—and breath whooshed out of his mouth.

His onscreen features moved.

"This is not something I meant to do. Hear that? I didn't mean it. I was mad and upset. My mother—a wonderful person—had just told me she'd filed for divorce because my father was having *another* affair. After he'd promised her he'd stop. Yeah, right. He would never stop. That man loves nobody but himself." Aaron's jaw worked. "It was January eighth, 2014. We were in a restaurant in Los Angeles. After dinner, I got in the car. It was dark, and I was still furious. I got lost trying to get back to the hotel. My anger made me go too fast, I admit it. I swerved onto a narrow residential street." Aaron shook his head. "I didn't even *see* the guy! Next thing I knew, I'd hit something. And then I saw the body fly. I ... my mind just exploded. I never meant ... I just floored it and got out of there. On the way into the hotel parking garage, I hit a pole to hide the damage on the car. I never heard what happened to the person I hit. The next day I flew back home to Texas." Aaron closed his eyes. "I'm done."

The scene froze on his rigid face.

Aaron's self-centered rage cost a man his life. Aaron Wang is WRATH.

"What?" Craig turned on Aaron, disbelief flattening his forehead. "You're the one who hit Nate?"

Aaron paled. "It *was* Nate? I wasn't sure. And I didn't mean to."

"*You. Killed. Nate?*"

Tori pressed her hands to her chest. "You're not just Wrath, you're a murderer!"

"Who's Nate?" Shari was totally lost. And she'd gotten a third one *wrong*.

The room exploded. Craig shoved Aaron, knocking him to the floor, and Tori yelled, and Lance yelled, and Shari heard herself shrieking "Stop it, stop it!", and Gina was pointing at the camera, screaming it was all George Fry's fault, and what was he trying to do? And in the back of Shari's mind, she knew she would be next, bare-faced on the screen, telling what she'd done, and the whole world would be watching …

Shari sank to the floor, panic bending her ribs. "*What is happening, who is Nate, please don't show me next, please, you said you wouldn't!*"

"Wait, wait!" Lance's voice.

Abrupt silence.

Shari looked up. Everyone had frozen where they were, eyes on the monitor. There on the screen—*her* face. Hair all messy, lips stretched wide, black mascara smeared down her cheeks. Looking awful. *Ugly.*

She went numb.

The picture on the monitor moved, and Shari heard her own panicked voice.

"Here's my confession. In May of 2012 I learned my mom had cancer and needed me. Even though it would hurt my career, I left California the very next day to go back home and nurse her. But I … before I heard about my mom, I was already in a really low spot. I'd tried out for so many parts and couldn't get them. I had to work odd jobs and could barely pay my bills." Shari pressed her lips. "The worst part was when my roommate, Kathryn Flex, got the part I wanted in *Last Bend*. I just felt so horrible, especially when they told me I was their second choice. I came *so* close …" Shari gulped. "I told some guy I'd dated a few times about it—and he said he could fix it. I … knew what he meant, and I … I'm sorry. I'm so sorry." Tears rolled down Shari's cheeks. "I told him to go ahead, do it." Her face crumbled. "I wasn't thinking straight. I'm not really like that, not at all! The very next day Kathryn was attacked outside our apartment building. It took her months to get better, and she lost the part." Shari wiped her cheeks. Her voice rose. "But I still didn't get the part, see? Because I chose to go help my mom. I chose *her* over *myself*. I'm not a bad person ..."

The monitor stilled on Shari's messed-up face, her eyes glittering and her mouth curled.

Shari Steele is ENVY.

I am not, I am not, I am not!

Gina lifted a hand to her mouth. "You did that to your *roommate*? Paid somebody to beat her up?"

"I didn't pay anybody! I didn't really think he'd do it."

"Yes, you did." Tori looked beyond disgusted. "I knew you were Envy, but *this* ... You should rot in hell."

"What does it matter?" Shari pushed to her feet, swaying. "She got a big movie in the end, didn't she? Now she's *famous*."

Lance and Craig stared at Shari with pure disdain.

Aaron curled his lip. "At least *I* didn't mean to hurt anybody."

Shari's back jammed straight. "Well, at least she's not *dead*!" She pivoted toward the monitor. "Get me off there!"

The screen went blank.

Shari couldn't *breathe*. She wanted to run, run, run — to the end of the earth and never be seen again. She *wasn't* a bad person!

The monitor lightened again. Lance's big face appeared, defeat stamped all over it.

"No." Lance saw himself and raised his palms. "*Don't. Please.*"

The picture rolled into motion.

"I only did it to protect my son. I'm a *father*. That's what fathers do. Scott got into some trouble at work. He stole fifty thousand dollars — purely on impulse. He's not a bad kid. He was only twenty-two! Just imagine if he was sent to some prison. I couldn't ... I *wouldn't* let that happen. All he needed was an alibi for the time of the robbery. I knew Bruce Egan would give him one, if I just paid him a little money. Bruce had reverted to using drugs again, and he was desperate. So he took the cash and told the lie to police. And my son, a *good kid*, was saved because of it. I never thought Douglas West, the young man Scott worked with, would be accused of the theft. But by then Bruce's story was set, and he was forced to repeat it in court. I hoped Douglas would be found innocent, truly I did. I never meant for him to go to jail. But once he was convicted, what could I do? And Scott certainly couldn't give the cash back."

The scene froze on Lance's chalk white face.

Lance and his son used stolen money to vacation in the Caribbean—and he wants millions more so he and his son need never work again. Lance Haslow is SLOTH.

Shari gaped at the monitor. He'd sent an innocent man to *jail*? And she'd gotten another sin wrong! "Lance is *Wrath*!" she screamed at a camera. "He attacked me twice!"

"The defendant was Douglas West?" Tori looked horrified.

"*You're* the reason that witness lied?" Craig's voice rose. *You* sent Doug to jail?"

Lance looked from Craig to Tori. "What—you know him?"

"He's Nate's brother!" Craig yelled. "Doug's conviction is one of the reasons Nate got so depressed. The second was *her*." He jabbed a finger at Tori.

Wait, what? Shari could hardly think anymore. Tori and Nate? And Lance and Nate? And Aaron? And Craig?

Shari spread her arms. "*Who* is Nate?"

"Craig's accountant," Gina said.

"But." Shari shook her head, her brain rattling. "Why is this all about *him*?"

Everybody stopped and gawked at her, like it was the first smart thing she'd ever said.

In her peripheral vision, Shari saw the monitor change.

"Wait, look." Gina pointed at the screen.

Text appeared. Tori stiffened.

After suffering through depression, two suicide attempts, and a divorce when her husband left her, Tori vowed she would never again be used by any man. Instead she used them, seducing one after the other. Tori Hattinger is Lust.

"That's ridiculous." Tori tossed her head. "Just because I've dated more than one man?"

"Hah!" Shari turned a triumphant look on her. "I *knew* it."

But it was the only one she'd gotten right. The *only* one.

"I got two right," Gina said.

"Me too." Lance tapped his notebook.

"I have *three*." Tori gave them a patronizing smile. "So there."

Shari's throat closed. She'd *lost*?

Gina's expression crumbled. "Four of you are going to jail! And Tori—you see what she's like. *I* should win."

"Give it up, Gina," Aaron seethed.

Shari saw the words on the monitor disappear. She raised a shaking finger to point at the screen, knowing what she'd see next, begging to be wrong.

The winner of Dream Prize is Tori Hattinger.

"Ahh!" Tori lifted her hands in the air. "Yes. Yes! Wow!"

Shari's legs gave out. She sat down hard on the floor.

Lance stumbled over to a couch. Aaron leaned against the table, his head down. Craig stared out the window, blank-faced.

Shari put her head in her hands. Gina was right. Craig and Aaron, Lance and her—they'd be arrested. Go to prison.

Shari Steele –in *prison*.

Why?

She pushed her head up, tears filling her eyes. This was so *wrong*.

"Who *are* you, George Fry? Why did you do this?"

"Shari's right." Lance stared at his feet, his voice lifeless. "This is about Nate."

But who cared about him, he was *dead*.

Craig tipped his head toward a camera. "Is that true, Fry? *Tell* us!"

"He won't tell you anything." Lance shook his head.

Tori laced and unlaced her hands, smiling to herself, shimmering with excitement. Wasn't she just happy as a clam.

"I don't have *anything* to do with Nate!" Gina was crying again, wringing her hands like some actress in a B movie.

What was she so worried about? At least she didn't have a horrible confession splatted in front of the entire world.

"Yes you do, indirectly." Aaron looked up, realization on his face. "You had an affair with my father. My mother told me about it at dinner, which made me furious. I drove off and hit Nate."

Gina shook her head. "I ..." Her mouth worked, then clamped shut, as if she was fighting with herself over what to say. She turned away.

Craig's face creased. "You're right, Aaron. And Tori treated Nate badly. And Lance got his brother wrongly convicted."

Shari pressed a hand against her forehead. This was insane. "*I* didn't have anything to do with that guy."

"And I only helped him!" Craig raised his arms. "I gave him a job!"

"You stole to start your foundation." Lance rubbed his face. "Maybe if he'd never worked for you he wouldn't have met Tori. Or gone to dinner that night."

"That's crazy! Those things aren't *my* fault!" Craig's face reddened. "You all did these things to him. I was his *friend*."

"And *I* never knew him." Shari glared at the camera. "I'm not—"

The words died in her throat.

The camera's green light was gone. *Gone.*

She scrambled to her feet. "Look." She pointed at the camera. Then swiveled to the second one in the room. The third. The fourth.

All were dark.

No, no, she still had things to say for herself! Explanations for what she did.

Dumbfounded, she gazed from Craig to Tori to Aaron to Lance. All of them looked like she felt. Abandoned. Dead.

What would happen to them now?

"And that's a wrap." Tori's voice lilted.

Shari burst into tears.

"Hello!"

A man's voice called from outside. She glanced up, blurry-eyed.

The sun-wrinkled boat captain appeared on the deck. He stepped through the sliding door, momentarily stilled by everyone's expressions.

"Hope you've had a pleasant stay. Now it's time for a boat ride."

Chapter 50

On the boat no one spoke, sitting as far from each other as possible. Tori stole glances at the other contestants. They remained stricken, staring into the distance. Gina couldn't stop crying, no doubt envisioning the end of her marriage. Remorse crimped her face, as if she'd do anything to erase the truths about herself the last three days had revealed. But some other emotion hung about her as well. It almost looked like … peace.

Tori had to be reading that one wrong.

As for Shari, Lance, Craig, and Aaron, they all wore tattered expressions of hopelessness. Surely they were imagining their inevitable years of punishment.

All five of them were facing ruined lives. Only Tori had survived.

Her reputation may be a little tarnished upon her return. But no one would dare accost her with any of this. Her personal life remained her own business. And never had it interfered with work. Besides, in comparison with the other people on this boat, she was a saint.

Tori watched the island grow small in the distance.

George Fry was manipulative and cunning. But that's exactly the kind of man it would take to make her dream of becoming President and CEO of *Serros* a reality. Tori understood now why the producer had been so intrigued with her choice of prize. It would present another challenge for him. Another scheme.

Perhaps he'd known from the beginning she would win.

Gina looked up and caught Tori's eye. There it was again in her gaze. That sense of ... something.

"What are you thinking?" Tori heard the words spill from her own mouth. As if she really cared.

Surprise flitted across Gina's forehead. When she spoke, her voice was steady, despite her tears. "I'm thinking how amazing it is that we allow ourselves to invite God's judgment when we could be walking in His mercy."

Huh?

Tori frowned. This show had clearly pushed Gina beyond her resources. The woman was downright addled.

Gina watched Tori, as if waiting for a response. When none came, she turned away.

Fine with me.

Tori smiled to herself, breathing in the ocean air, reveling in the sun on her skin.

Forget Gina and all the rest of them. The last three days had been tough, but Tori had prevailed. She'd done it all on her own and *won*. More victories lay ahead.

She'd need to find a new young man to help her celebrate.

Wednesday, March 9

Epilogue

Such a beautiful piece of property.

Too bad he hadn't been able to enjoy it.

Wind dried the sweat on the producer's forehead as he slowed the boat's motor and watched the island draw near. Only eight o'clock in the morning, and the day had dawned hotter than usual. It would be a tiring day of hard work. But a victorious one.

When the bow scraped sand he turned off the engine and dropped the rear anchor.

He splashed through the ankle deep water almost like a kid. Thank God it was Wednesday. Had it been only last Saturday that he'd readied everything for the show? It seemed like an eternity.

But it had *worked*. He'd made it all happen.

Justice.

He closed his eyes and tipped his face upward, feeling the sun on his face.

Quickly he crossed the sand and started on the uphill path to the house. Then through the gate and across the deck. The sliding glass doors and curtains were open to all the bedrooms. He stopped at the first one and peered inside. He saw the bed and other furniture, but nothing else. All the equipment was gone.

His tech whiz assistant had been busy.

He found Sam upstairs in the great room at the center table. "Well, look who's here—'George Fry.'"

Sam laughed. "Yeah, without the itchy toupee. You're here early."

"Got an early start. I was awake hours ago. Hard to sleep."

"I'll bet." Sam walked over, arm outstretched. "Congratulations, boss."

They shook hands. Relief and vindication surged through the producer. "Thanks. Couldn't have done it without you." He looked around the all too familiar room. He could hardly believe it was over, after a solid year of planning.

Sam grinned. "Feels good, doesn't it."

"Feels amazing. Promises kept."

The producer stepped back. "Looks like you've been busy downstairs."

Sam nodded. "I got an early start, too. Began last night as soon as the house was empty and the boat out of sight. All the cameras and monitors from the bedrooms are packed up. Got the ones from the bunker, too. I was just about to pull up the cable from the main monitor here."

That was a lot of equipment he'd already dismantled. The producer's own bedroom had been stuffed with his personal camera plus ten screens that ran film from the bunker and various areas of the house.

"How about in your cabin?"

During the three days of filming Sam had been holed up in a cabin on the north side of the island, watching all the feeds on screens of his own and putting up the text and clues on the monitors. He'd been equipped with a boat in case of emergency.

"All that's still to do."

"No worries, we'll knock it out together."

Sam went back to work, pulling up the cord and wrapping it around the base of the monitor. The producer watched, remembering with a shudder the clues given on that screen. The sickening tension in the room. They deserved it, all five of those people. They deserved everything they'd gotten. When the monitor was ready, Sam carried it out to the deck and set it near the top of the curving steps. They'd haul it to the boat later.

He stepped back into the great room. "Okay, Craig. Time for the hard part."

The bunker.

"I've already got the shovels and tools out there. Plus the dirt and bushes."

"You *have* been busy."

They stopped in the kitchen for two water bottles, then went down the stairs and out the back door. Across the deck and through the forbidden gate. At the heavy door to the shed, Sam reached into his pocket. "I've got my fob." He brought it out and pressed the button. The door unlocked.

Craig pulled it open and peered down the dark stairway. He shivered.

"Memories?"

He nodded.

For a claustrophobic, locking himself in that bunker had been the hardest thing he'd ever done, even though his own fob lay in his pocket. Half of the choking he suffered in that death hole hadn't been faked.

He took a deep breath. "Let's get to it."

With gloved hands they began tearing down the shed.

As Craig worked, faces and voices from the past two years pulsed in his memories. He thought of that fateful day Nate had not shown up for work *again*. How Craig had thought he would have to fire him—only to learn within the hour that Nate was clinging to life in a hospital, the victim of a hit and run. Craig had been at Nate's side as he died, vowing through clenched teeth to find who hit him. Good-hearted Nate hadn't even cared about that.

"Just get my brother out of jail," he whispered.

So much evil in this world. So much for Craig to fix. He'd already put his millions to work, helping struggling victims of M.S. After Nate's death Craig spent whatever it took to keep his promises. Sam Jefferson's months of dogged and brilliant detective work had been worth every penny.

The first two walls of the shed were knocked flat. Craig started on the third.

His mind turned to Kathryn Flex. How humble and down to earth she'd been when he met her at a party, even after her sky rocket to fame. She'd become a good friend. He could still see her face as she told him about the attack she'd suffered, her suspicions of who'd been behind it. But the police could find no evidence.

This, too, Craig had now made right.

People talked of a God who cared about injustice. Sure. Where had *He* been?

Together Sam and Craig began demolition on the last wall.

"Those confessions were incredible, man." Sam swung his hammer. "My mouth just dropped open, listening to them."

"Yeah. And didn't they have an excuse for everything." Craig's tone turned mocking. "'We're good people, really, we never meant it.'"

"Sure hope you're right about the confessions holding up in court." Sam used his T-shirt to wipe sweat from his face.

Craig laughed. "I'd love to see the defense lawyers try to argue against them. Made under duress? In some reality show and bunker that never existed? Riiight."

He pictured the five "contestants" catching their flights home, stomachs roiling over what they'd find when they landed. How stunned they'd be to learn there had never been a *Dream Prize* show on T.V. Tori had won nothing. No website for the supposed show or the fake Sensation Network remained. Even the footprint for buying those domains had been erased.

The shed's walls and door lay on the ground. Sam started a chain saw. As he cut the wood into pieces, Craig chucked them down the grungy stairwell.

Maybe Tori and Gina would learn their lesson. With no record of their selfish choices laid bare to the world, they could resume their lives, changed women. But Craig doubted that for Tori. She'd likely just be furious to learn she'd been duped. Gina—maybe. As they'd gotten off the boat on the mainland, she actually told Aaron she was sorry. Not that he'd accepted her apology.

As for Aaron, Lance, and Shari, their relief would be short lived. Their anonymously sent confessions would soon land on the desks of the detectives who'd investigated their crimes, and the reporters who'd covered the stories.

Sam turned off the chainsaw and rested for a minute. Craig sat down and guzzled his water.

"That Shari's got no acting talent on you." Sam picked up his own bottle. "Your 'confession' was great."

Craig smirked. As if he, with his hundred million dollar trust fund, would ever need to steal anyone else's money.

"And that first day in the kitchen, when you described the three supposed pictures in your room? The *look* on

Shari's face when you mentioned *Upside Out*." Sam laughed.

It had rattled her, all right.

"I couldn't wait to make those people suffer," Craig said. "Just being in a house with them for three days ..."

"Gina almost got *you*, though, when she realized who you were. Scared me for a minute."

"Gina's not as smart as she thinks she is."

In the planning stages, Craig had gone back and forth regarding using his real name. His final decision arose from the fear that in the future one of the others might see a picture of him at some news-covered event. If the caption read a different name, would they grow suspicious? Better to let them think he'd been duped, as they had been.

"Wouldn't it be funny"—Craig finished the last of his water—"if one of them tried to accuse me publicly of the embezzlement?"

"That would be funny, all right."

Even more ridiculous? Deigning to label himself as Pride.

They threw their empty bottles down the stairwell and got back to work.

By the time the pieces of wood were all cut and thrown down, the stairwell was nearly full. Together, Sam and Craig lifted the heavy trap door over the opening and banged it shut.

Next—covering the area. They walked farther down the path to fetch waiting bags of dirt, which they dragged back and spread on top of the trap door, deep enough for planting. Then they prepared three holes and planted the bushes that awaited in pots.

When they were done, Craig and Sam stood back and admired their work.

"What bunker?" Sam spread his hands.

They looked at each other and grinned.

Back at the house they took time for lunch, lolling on the deck and watching the ocean as they ate. After that they packed up all the equipment in the cabin and loaded everything onto Craig's rented boat. The other boat would remain on the island. It and the entire property would soon be sold in the same way he'd bought it — through a dummy corporation that could not be traced to Craig.

On the mainland his jet stood ready to fly them home.

Sam drove the boat away from the *Dream Prize* island. Craig watched the house recede, remembering his arrival with the others just three days ago. Hateful, self-centered people. So focused on their own vain empires.

Sinners, they were. Sinners, all.

Discussion Questions

1. With what character did you identify the most? Why?

2. How did you read this complex story? Did you simply allow things to be revealed as you read, or did you take notes and actively try to figure out the puzzle? How much of the puzzle did you guess before all was revealed?

3. How did the aura of judgment without mercy effect the characters' relationships with themselves? With each other? With nature?

4. Gina said she'd asked God for forgiveness for the sin she'd committed. Yet she continues to deny publicly she ever committed that sin and particularly wants to hide it from her husband, who would be hurt to learn the truth. Is she wrong to do this?

5. Gina says this to George Fry: "Nobody represents just one sin. We're all sinners before God—that's what the Bible says. At one time or another everybody on earth— including you—has probably committed all the Seven

Deadly Sins. Who are you to decide what we are?" Do you agree with this statement?

6. What passages did you underline or highlight as "quotable quotes?"

7. How many characters and sins did you match correctly? In the end, did it matter which sin the producer matched to each character?

8. In Chapter 46, Gina has this sudden thought: *What if God was trying to help, and she hadn't been listening? What if, even in experiencing His mercy for her sin, there may still be consequences to pay? Would she be willing to do whatever God asked of her, walk in His truth? Or would she go her own way again?* What do you think about this?

9. In Chapter 49 after the judgments, Shari is still trying to explain her actions to the cameras, only to realize they've all been turned off. Does this passage hold any symbolism for you? If so, what?

10. "Now it's time for a boat ride." For readers knowledgeable in Greek mythology, what was the symbolism of these words spoken by the boat captain at the end of chapter 49, after the judgments had been pronounced?

11. Did you guess the twist at the end of the story? Looking back through the book, what were the clues that pointed to this twist?

12. What is the theme of this novel?

13. What life lessons did you take away from this book?

Read the first chapters of all Brandilyn Collins'
books at her website:
www.brandilyncollins.com

Connect with her on Facebook:
www.facebook.com/brandilyncollinsseatbeltsuspense

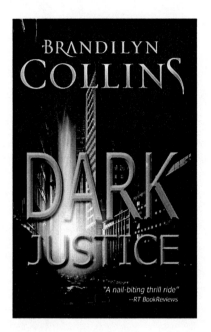

If I'd had any idea what those words would mean to me, to my mother and daughter, I'd have fled California without looking back.

While driving a rural road, Hannah Shire and her aging mother, who suffers from dementia, stop to help a man at the scene of a car accident. The man whispers mysterious words in Hannah's ear. Soon people want to kill Hannah and her mother for what they "know." Even law enforcement may be involved.

The two women must flee for their lives. But how does Hannah hide her confused mother? Carol just wants to listen to her pop music, wear her favorite purple hat, and go home. And if they turn to Hannah's twenty-seven-year-old daughter, Emily, for help, will she fall into danger as well?

Pressed on all sides, Hannah must keep all three generations of women in her family alive. Only then does she learn the threat is not just to her loved ones, but the entire country.

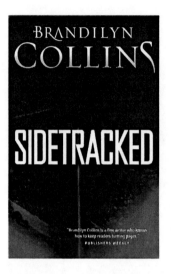

When you live a lie for so long, it becomes a part of you. Like clothing first rough and scratchy, it eventually wears down, thins out. Sinks into your skin.

Thirty-four-year-old Delanie Miller has fled her dark past and is now settled into a quiet life in small-town Kentucky. She has friends, a faux "family" who lives in her house, and a loving boyfriend who may soon ask her to marry him. Her aching dream of a husband and future children are about to come true. But protecting this life of promise means keeping a low profile and guarding the truth of her past—from *everyone*.

The town's peace is shattered when Delanie's friend, Clara, is murdered, and Delanie finds her body. The police chief quickly zeroes in on Billy King, a simple-minded young man whom Delanie knows would never hurt Clara. Delanie can hunt down evidence and speak out publicly against the chief— only at great risk of her own exposure. But after suffering such injustice in her own past, how can she keep silent now? Delanie must find a way to uncover Clara's murderer yet save the life she's created for herself—the deceit-ridden life that will forever distance her from others and God.

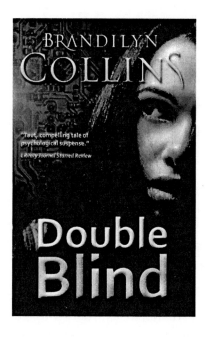

Desperate people make desperate choices.

Twenty-nine-year-old Lisa Newberry can barely make it through the day. Suddenly widowed and a survivor of a near-fatal attack, she is wracked with grief and despair. Then she hears of a medical trial for a tiny brain chip that emits electrical pulses to heal severe depression. At rope's end, Lisa offers herself as a candidate.

When she receives her letter of acceptance for the trial, Lisa is at first hopeful. But—*brain surgery.* Can she really go through with that? What if she receives only the placebo?

What if something far worse goes wrong?

Written in the relentless style for which Brandilyn Collins is known, *Double Blind* is a psychological thriller with mind-bending twists. Lisa faces choices that drive her to the brink, and one wrong move could cost the lives of many.

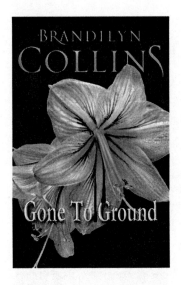

BRANDILYN COLLINS

COLLINS

Gone To Ground

Amaryllis, Mississippi is a scrappy little town of strong backbone and southern hospitality. A brick-paved Main Street, a park, and the legendary ghost in its ancient cemetery are all part of its heritage. Everybody knows everybody in Amaryllis, and gossip wafts on the breeze. Its denizens are friendly, its families tight. On the surface Amaryllis seems much like the flower for which it's named — bright and fragrant.

But the Amaryllis flower is poisonous.

In the past three years five unsolved murders have occurred within the town. All the victims were women, killed in similar fashion in their homes. And two nights ago — a sixth victim.

Clearly a killer lives and breathes among the good citizens of Amaryllis. And now three terrified women are sure they know who he is — someone close to them. None is aware of the others' suspicions. Independently, each woman must make the heartrending choice to bring the killer down.

But each suspects a different man.

CPSIA information can be obtained
at www.ICGtesting.com
Printed in the USA
LVOW12s0417011116

511104LV00001B/24/P